Yates's Dilemma

When Wendell Moon hightailed it out of Monotony, he left in his wake a murdered lawman and a mob braying for his blood. Fifteen years later the word is out – Wendell Moon is back! But for Sheriff Cassidy Yates, Wendell's unwelcome return rekindles old vendettas and ignites three days of raging gun battles.

Now the sheriff has the impossible duty of keeping the peace, but as if that isn't enough Wendell also claims he never killed the lawman.

If Cassidy doesn't unearth the truth quickly, Wendell's trigger-happy enemies will deliver their own form of gun-toting justice. Real trouble lies ahead!

Yates's Dilemma

I. J. PARNHAM

A Black Horse Western

ROBERT HALE · LONDON

© I. J. Parnham 2004
First published in Great Britain 2004

ISBN 0 7090 7464 6

Robert Hale Limited
Clerkenwell House
Clerkenwell Green
London EC1R 0HT

Typeset by
Derek Doyle & Associates, Liverpool.
Printed and bound in Great Britain by
Antony Rowe Limited, Wiltshire

CHAPTER 1

On Trinity's main drag four men stood before the town's only hotel, their long coats rippling in the cool, evening breeze. Each man was grizzled and dirty. Long years of harsh weather had tanned their faces to dull leather.

They shared nods, then clumped on to the board-walk. The tallest man, Zachary Forester, pulled his hat low so that it nestled above his cold eyes, then pushed through the hotel's door.

He swaggered to the reception desk, clumping his boots on the hardwood floor with deliberate paces.

The receptionist, Dexter, looked up. He gulped.

'What can I do for you four gentlemen?' he asked.

Zachary grinned, a streak of ice amid the bristles and grime.

'Get me Wendell Moon,' he muttered, his voice low and gravelly.

Dexter rubbed his sweating palms on his jacket.

'Mr Moon is a popular man in Trinity. He gave explicit instructions that he is not seeing visitors this late.'

5

'Is that so?'

'It is.' Dexter placed his pen in the centre of his reservations book. He fluffed the potted palm on the desk and ran a long finger along the nearest frond of a huge aspidistra. 'And as he isn't here for long, he can't see everyone that wants an audience.'

'An audience.' Zachary glanced back at his associates, who all snorted a humourless chuckle. 'I don't want an audience.'

'Then what do you want?'

With a move like lightning Zachary grabbed Dexter's collar and dragged him across the desk, Dexter's flailing arms crashing the plants to the floor.

'I want to see Wendell Moon. Now!'

Dexter wheezed. He batted his fists against Zachary's firm hand but finding no give, he slumped and gave the smallest of nods.

For ten seconds Zachary held on, then threw him back behind the desk.

Dexter smoothed his ruffled jacket and grabbed his reservations book. He riffled through to the last page, swivelled it round, and jammed a finger beside a name.

'I am not allowed to say which room Mr Moon is in,' he said, raising his voice. He waggled his eyebrows and looked down at his finger.

Zachary glanced at the finger, then slammed both fists on the desk.

'Don't belittle me,' he roared, thrusting his face to within inches of Dexter's. 'Where is Wendell?'

Dexter backed. He blinked twice, gulping.

'Mr Moon is in room eleven,' he said, his voice

shaking. 'It's on the second floor. An eleven has two straight lines with—'

'Enough,' Zachary muttered, turning from the desk. He stormed to the stairs and mounted them four at a time.

Behind him, Dexter grumbled to himself as he rescued the plants from the floor, then silenced when the other three men glared at him.

On the second-floor landing Zachary paced back and forth. While the others clumped up the stairs, he drew his gun. He threw open the barrel, confirmed he had six bullets loaded, and threw it closed.

When his men joined him on the landing, they did likewise. Lester Jameson pushed to the front.

'I'll lead,' he said.

'You ain't,' Zachary snapped, slamming Lester back against the wall. 'I've waited fifteen years for this – nobody will deny me.'

Lester glared back, then nodded.

Zachary stalked down the corridor, glaring at each of the passing doors until he reached room eleven. While his men took positions on either side of him, he took long, deep breaths and rolled his shoulders.

Each man hunched their shoulders and thrust their guns straight out.

Zachary kicked open the door.

The door slammed back against the wall and rebounded, Zachary catching it with his left hand. He stood with his gun aimed into the room, then swung around the door, dropping to his haunches and aiming at the bed.

The bed was empty – as was the rest of the room.

With an angry snort, Zachary stalked inside, his men following.

Lester dashed through the room. He peered under the bed, threw open cupboard doors and rifled through the drawers, but Zachary only had eyes for the open window.

There, the curtains billowed.

One steady pace at a time he stalked to the window, his gun held upright, the cold metal brushing his right cheek. The veranda appeared.

With an assured lunge he swung outside and glanced left and right.

The veranda was unoccupied.

He swung back in, gritting his teeth.

As he forced his anger to subside, he slammed his fist against his thigh, then holstered his gun. He rolled his tongue around his mouth and spat a long stream of spit on the floor.

He smiled.

A plate rested on the bedside table – and a cigar smouldered on it.

He strode to the table, considering the cigar's rising funnel of smoke. He lifted the cigar and sniffed the acrid fumes.

With an angry lunge he ground the cigar into crumbled leaves.

'We're getting closer,' he whispered.

CHAPTER 2

On the edge of his twenty-acre field Stirling Fontana
leaned back and rubbed the base of his back, knead-
ing his aged muscles. He glanced around. His wrin-
kled face snarled into a frown.

From down the trail a rider approached, his gait
slow.

With a casual gesture Stirling grabbed his pitchfork. He stabbed it into the ground and leaned on it
while peering at the rider. He narrowed his eyes to
slits, trying to compensate for his failing eyesight.

Then for the first time a smile broke through and
he lifted his hat to wave it.

The rider waved back.

'Howdy, Jackson,' Stirling hollered.

The rider, Jackson, pulled his horse from the trail
and paced on to the field. He halted beside Stirling
and nodded.

'Howdy.' Jackson looked around. 'This is a fine
stretch of land.'

Stirling beamed, etching his face in deep wrinkles.
'It is.'

'Barley?'

'Wheat.'

Jackson smiled. 'Of course it is.'

In silence they contemplated each other.

Stirling hung his head a moment. 'I'm guessing you ain't come to see me for the first time in fifteen years to discuss farming.'

Jackson sighed, the sound tired. 'I ain't.'

Stirling rubbed his chin. He wheezed a deep breath and patted Jackson's bay on the head. He looked up at Jackson.

'Have you found him?' he whispered.

Jackson spat to the side. 'Yup. Wendell Moon is back.'

Stirling kicked his pitchfork to the ground. With his breath coming in short gasps, he glared at the fallen tool for long moments. When his breathing slowed he nodded to Jackson.

'Then I'll get my gun.' Without further comment Stirling strode to the trail and with his head down, headed for his farmhouse.

Behind him, Jackson hollered and Stirling glanced back.

From further down the trail, two riders emerged from under a bur oak.

Stirling produced a thin smile, pleased that at least they were still alive. He hurried to a fast walk. As he entered his small farmyard the riders flanked him.

All three men dismounted. Each man was about Stirling's age, the long years heavy on their stooped shoulders and spreading waistlines, but in their eyes a cold determination festered.

Stirling shook their hands. Nobody said a word.

None of them needed to say anything.

Katherine Fontana emerged from the farmhouse, her face wreathed in a big smile, which disappeared as soon as she saw Jackson and the others.

'This doesn't look like a social call,' she muttered, her lips thin.

Stirling lifted his hat to rub a hand through his thinning hair. He replaced the hat and held his hands wide.

'I ain't looking for an argument.'

Katherine folded her arms. 'Didn't say you'd get one.'

They stared at each other. Stirling patted her shoulder, then edged past her and strode into the house.

Katherine sighed, contemplating the three men.

'Who found him?' she asked.

The eldest and thinnest of the men, Wayne Stone, lifted a hand.

'I did,' he said. He removed his half-glasses and rubbed them on his sleeve. 'I still have plenty of contacts from the Mississippi to the Pacific. One of them contacted me to say Wendell Moon had passed through and he was heading east.'

Katherine raised her eyebrows. 'You reckon he's coming here?'

Wayne shook his head. 'Word was he's heading to Monotony and then on to Redemption City. We'll get him in one place or the other.'

Katherine shook her head. 'Your contact must be wrong. Wendell wouldn't return to Monotony – not

11

even after fifteen years.'

The youngest of the group, Frank Taylor, snorted.

'Wendell liked risks and he liked rubbing people's noses in his *supposed* superiority. It doesn't seem odd to me that he'd return there.' Frank patted his holster. 'Except it's the last place he'll see.'

'Katherine,' Jackson said, 'from what you're saying, you have no objection to Stirling joining us?'

'I spent twelve years married to a man with a star, and I hated what he did. I've enjoyed the last ten more, but I ain't objecting to him joining you.' Katherine sighed. 'I knew Ruth McAlister.'

Jackson gulped, his eyes glazing with an old, painful memory.

They stood in silence until Stirling emerged, his eldest son, Henry, following behind.

Stirling bustled with his saddle-bag, then nodded to Henry.

'Henry, you're in charge of the farm while I'm gone. This is your big chance to show me what you can do.' He narrowed his eyes, then winked. 'Don't disappoint me.'

Henry leaned forward, his youthful eyes bright, his gangling form eager.

'Is it Wendell Moon you're going after?' he asked.

Stirling sneered. 'Yup.'

'And are these the men you used to ride with?' Henry pointed to the arc of men. 'Jackson Wilson, Frank Taylor and—'

'Wayne Stone,' Stirling said. 'And we only rode together once.'

12

Henry licked his lips. 'Then I'll get my rifle. This will be—'

'You're doing nothing,' Stirling shouted. He grabbed Henry's shoulder as the youngster turned to the house.

Henry squirmed from Stirling's grip. 'You've told me about Wendell Moon and what he did all my life. I—'

'You're doing nothing, boy,' Stirling muttered. 'Except staying here and looking after the farm with your ma.'

'But you said that if I were old enough, I could ride with you.'

'But nothing.'

Stirling slapped Henry's cheek for him to sprawl back against the wall and fall to his knees.

Henry leapt to his feet, his fists bunched, a wetness in his eyes. He rolled back and forth on his heels, then with a grunted oath, scurried inside the house.

'Language, boy.' Stirling moved to follow him in, but Katherine grabbed his arm.

'Don't,' she said. 'I'll explain to him.'

'Obliged.' Stirling lowered his head. 'But I shouldn't have hit him.'

'He knows you ain't angry with him. But it stopped that madness.'

Stirling nodded. He glanced at the others.

Everyone returned embarrassed smiles, then mounted their horses. They turned and rode from the farm at a walking pace.

Stirling turned to Katherine and met her gaze.

'I . . . I know that. . . .'

'We have nothing to say,' Katherine said. 'Just go. This is the last of your lawman duties. Once this is over, you have nothing left of your former life.'

'This ain't nothing to do with being a lawman.'

'I know that too. Now just go.'

Stirling kissed her cheek, clutching her shoulders, then tore himself away and strode to his horse. With a last holler he trotted after the others. He resisted the urge to look back, judging that it wouldn't help either him or Katherine.

'Anyone objecting if I lead?' he asked when he drew alongside, his voice more gruff than normal.

'We wouldn't have it any other way,' Wayne said. 'What's your plan?'

'We keep it simple. We head him off in Monotony and sort this.' Stirling sighed as he considered Wayne's stooped form, the length of bony arm protruding from his sleeve, the deep wrinkles etching his face. 'Ain't my place to say this, but are you sure you want to come with us?'

Wayne pushed his half-glasses further up his angular nose.

'What you mean?'

'I mean that time ain't been that kind to you. An old-timer might just get himself hurt – and Wendell Moon has ruined enough good men.'

'Old-timer,' Wayne muttered. 'You obviously ain't looked at yourself for some years – not that I can blame you.'

Frank and Jackson chuckled, Stirling joining in after a moment.

'I ain't insulting you, but you were a judge. You

didn't live with a gun, and now ain't the time to start trying to use one.'

Wayne nodded. 'I hear you, but we swore an oath.'

With that question answered the riders returned to silence, each man lost in his own brooding thoughts. At a steady pace they trudged into the hills, their shadows lengthening behind them.

Long after they'd left Stirling's farm and, with dusk shrouding the hills in gathering darkness, a lone rider followed their trail.

The rider's frame was gawky. Every few paces he checked the strapping on his rifle. He also glanced over his shoulder as much as forward.

But with every pace away from the farm, his back straightened a little more.

CHAPTER 3

'Is this Wendell Moon telling the truth?' James Whittler asked.

Sheriff Cassidy Yates chuckled. This wasn't the first time someone had asked him that question. This morning, Monotony's newly arrived businessman was the only topic everybody wanted to discuss and now James Whittler had come into his office to continue the gossiping.

Cassidy leaned back in his chair and folded his hands behind his head.

'The way I see it, there's two possibilities.'

'That's what everyone says. I've only met his attorney, but he gave me a draft copy of the legal papers. Wendell's offered me two dollars an acre.'

'And what do you reckon your land is worth?'

'Paid a dollar for it.'

'Then I reckon it's a good deal.'

James rubbed his chin and sat on the edge of Cassidy's desk.

'Yeah, but I'm wondering if he's being as generous as he seems.'

Cassidy snorted and shook his head. 'You farmers are all the same. If he'd offered you fifty cents, you'd say he's conning you. If he'd offered you a dollar, you'd say it's worth two. But he's offered you two, so why are you complaining?'

'The way I see it, his *apparently* generous offer means he reckons the railroad will increase land prices. And he might be right.'

'The railroad might not reach us or it might miss us. Then your land won't even be worth the dollar you paid for it. Wendell is a speculator, who reckons he can make a profit, but he's taking all the risks.'

'You're a gambling man, Sheriff. Are you saying I should take the money?'

Cassidy rolled to his feet and leaned forward to place both hands flat on his desk.

'The nearest equivalent I can offer is that you've locked horns all night with four keen poker players and three have backed out of the biggest pot of the night. You're sitting with a king in the hole, making two pair and you. . . . Cutting it short, your opponent offers to split the pot. As five people filled the pot, you can walk away with a profit or risk getting a bigger profit against—'

'Walking away with nothing.' James sauntered to the window and looked outside at the Silver Streak Saloon opposite. 'So it still comes down to my first question – is this Wendell Moon telling the truth?'

Three days after leaving his farm, Stirling's group rode into Monotony.

In the early afternoon, laden carts trundled past

and the excited chatter of people going about their business echoed down the road. Fifteen years ago Monotony was just a stopping-off point on the trail. Now the approaching railroad had transformed this town. Everywhere windows shone, boardwalks were scrubbed and people were dressed smartly.

With widening eyes each man stared at the buildings, many of which were either newly built or freshly painted. When they passed the third saloon, Jackson tipped back his hat.

'Got to say this, Monotony sure has changed. Ain't been through here in twelve years and I wouldn't take much convincing that we'd come to the wrong place.'

Everyone produced low whistles and agreements. Stirling directed his group to the first hotel on the road and pulled up.

'Monotony's bigger than I thought,' he said. 'This might take some time. We need to ask around and find out if Wendell's arrived yet.'

'Yeah,' Frank muttered. 'The folk in that last trading post weren't cooperative.'

Stirling nodded. 'Wayne, take this side of the road. Frank, take the other. Me and Jackson will start at the other end – and be subtle.'

Everyone nodded but Wayne shook his head.

'Knew I came along for a reason,' he said, slotting his gnarled thumbs into his waistcoat. 'If I remember the last time we rode together correctly, you provided the decisions, Jackson provided the craftiness and Frank provided the firepower.'

'And what do you reckon you provided?'

By way of an answer Wayne tapped his forehead until everyone smiled. He swung his finger to the right and pointed to a grey mare standing outside the Silver Streak Saloon.

Stirling shook his head. 'Wendell rode a grey mare before, but that was fifteen years ago.'

'Horses may come and go, but the man you are doesn't change.'

Stirling shrugged, but Frank nodded.

'Even if Wayne's wrong,' he said, 'a saloon sounds a good place to start.'

Stirling glared at the grey mare, then swung from his horse, the other men following him.

Frank strode to the front. With the other three men flanking him, he strode on to the boardwalk and straight into the saloon. He hung on to the swing-doors as he glanced around the room.

This early in the afternoon only a few people sat inside – most were on their own, nursing coffees. But at the back of the saloon, four men sat around a table, talking.

The eldest of the men faced the wall. His former thin frame had thickened, bulges rolling over his waistband. Unkempt grey hair poked from beneath the Stetson but his trim clothes were pressed and clean.

Even after fifteen years, this was unmistakably Wendell Moon.

Wendell wasn't packing a gun but the other three men around the table were. Clad in sharp city suits, lean and hard-boned, they were clearly gunslingers. Each man glanced to the door from the corner of

19

their eyes, feigning indifference as they appraised Frank.

Frank winced when he saw that the gunslingers wore silver moon-shaped badges on their lapels. He pushed the swing-doors from him so they rattled against the doorframe, then strode inside. While the others filed in behind him, he stood hunched, his hands opening and closing.

The gunslingers shuffled on the chairs and leaned back to stare at Frank. One whispered something to Wendell, who stiffened, but still kept his back to the door and his face downturned.

Frank strode across the saloon straight for Wendell and swung to a standstill beside his table.

'Wendell J. Moon,' he muttered, his voice low.

'Yeah,' a gunslinger said. 'Who wants him?'

Frank glared down at the top of Wendell's Stetson.

'I wasn't speaking to you. I was speaking to Wendell.'

'And I want to know if Mr Moon wants to speak to you.'

'Mr Moon,' Frank snorted. He licked his lips. 'He will.'

Wendell's hat waggled, a low chuckle escaping.

'I reckon I know that voice,' he said, his tone light. 'Perhaps I do want to speak to you.'

Frank gritted his teeth. 'And *I* recognize that voice.'

Wendell looked up an inch at a time until his face emerged. Beneath the hat the cheeks were clean-shaven and the face glowed with health. But the blank eyes hadn't changed.

'You paying me a visit to share old memories?'

'Nope.'

Wendell shrugged. He glanced over his shoulder at Stirling and the others. His right eye twitched with the barest of winks. He turned back to Frank.

'Then what do you want?'

'I'm here to give you two choices. You can either die inside or come out into the road and die.'

The muted conversation within the saloon silenced. From an adjoining table, two men edged to their feet then dashed outside.

Wendell chuckled, the sound untroubled. 'And if I don't like those choices?'

Frank leaned down and forced his face into the grimmest of smiles.

'You'll just have to accept my decision.'

Wendell's gunslingers glared up at Frank, their bodies still, but their gazes lingered over Frank's spreading waistline and sagging jowls.

'I don't reckon you're still a lawman.' Wendell smiled. 'You're way too old.'

'Don't need to be a lawman to stamp out bugs like you.'

The swing-doors behind Frank slammed back against the wall. Firm footfalls paced into the room.

'I ain't standing for threats in my town,' someone muttered from behind Frank.

Frank glared down at Wendell a moment longer, then glanced over his shoulder.

A man with a star stood beside the door, his hand resting on his gunbelt.

Frank tipped his hat to him.

'You'll get no trouble from me, Sheriff.'

'Glad to hear it,' the sheriff said, 'because I'm sure Mr Moon doesn't want any.'

'Mr Moon,' Frank snapped with a snort, 'has no choice.'

The sheriff rolled his shoulders. 'That's your last threat, stranger. Now you'll leave.'

Frank glared back, then nodded. He glanced down at Wendell.

'Don't go anywhere,' he muttered from the corner of his mouth. He strode past his colleagues and the sheriff, who filed after him through the swing-doors.

Outside, Wayne patted Frank's shoulder.

'We came for Wendell,' he said, 'but whether we get him or he swings, it don't matter none.'

'Yeah.' Frank turned to watch the sheriff stride from the saloon. 'Sheriff, we'd like a word with you.'

The sheriff gestured across the road.

'Then you and I have the same idea. My office is this way.'

Without further comment they filed across the road to the sheriff's office. Once inside, the sheriff sauntered behind his desk. He sat and leaned back. With his hands behind his head, he threw his heels on the desk and considered Frank.

'Name's Cassidy Yates and you need to know one thing. For the six months I've been based in Monotony I've run a quiet town. If you accept that, we'll get on fine. If not. . . .'

Frank glanced through the window. 'I can see this is a fine town. We ain't here to cause you problems.'

'I'll accept your word. So what's your problem with Mr Moon?'

Frank grunted. 'Wendell is a two-bit, lousy snake.'

Cassidy winced. 'He's only been here a few hours but he's already introduced himself and he seems a regular businessman.'

'What's his business?'

'It ain't your concern, but as it's common knowledge – he's trying to buy James Whittler's land. He's offered him two dollars an acre, which I reckon is a more than fair price.'

'You ain't speaking sense. You're making out Wendell is a generous benefactor.'

'He might be or then again he might not be.' Cassidy shrugged. 'Either way, the townsfolk are glad he's around. Where his type goes, prosperity ain't far away. So what business deal are you complaining about?'

'No business deal,' Frank spat, 'just murder.'

'I'm sure Mr Moon would have nothing to do with that sort of thing. It'd be bad for business.' Cassidy clattered his feet down from the desk and leaned forward. 'But you'd better tell me the details. Where do you claim this happened?'

'In Monotony.'

'I ain't had any murders in the last six months.' Cassidy tipped back his hat to scratch his forehead. 'Can't remember any unsolved murders before that.'

'It happened fifteen years ago.'

'Fifteen years!' Cassidy blew out his cheeks. 'And you just happened to be passing through and you recognized Wendell after all those years?'

'We followed him here.'

'Men who bear a grudge that long need persuading to ignore that grudge, so I'll tell you again, I run a quiet town.'

'We don't need persuading. We're on the same side. We're ex-lawmen. I was Sheriff Frank Taylor.' Frank gestured to the left and right. 'Stirling Fontana was a sheriff too. Jackson Wilson was Prudence's town marshal. Wayne Stone was the judge in Beaver Ridge before Ronald Daniels took over. We're long retired but we ain't spent one second of our lives on the wrong side of the law.'

Cassidy sighed and ran a hand over his brow.

'In that case I suppose you'd better tell me about it.'

'Wendell Moon rode with the Forester gang. You'll have heard of them.'

'Nope.'

'They terrorized these parts one summer. Then Wendell turned on Zachary Forester and tried to run things himself, but Sheriff Ben McAlister – may his soul rest in peace – ran the whole lot of them out of town. But Wendell he ain't taken with Ben. He and the remnants of Forester's gang tracked him back to his home and killed him and his family.'

'You saw this?'

'Nope. We found the bodies four days later, and we swore an oath that—'

Cassidy lifted a hand. 'Four days later is no good. Lawmen make plenty of enemies, so what made you think Wendell killed them?'

'It *was* him.' Frank took a deep breath. 'We

24

tracked everyone else that was involved, but that devious snake Wendell escaped.'

'And did the men you tracked down confirm what they did?'

Frank chewed his bottom lip, suppressing a grin.

'They got just as many chances to explain themselves as Ben McAlister got.'

For long moments Cassidy stared at Frank. He sighed.

'You got any proof, aside from your word, that the businessman in the Silver Streak Saloon and this suspected murderer are the same man?'

'Ask around.' Frank pointed through the window. 'Plenty of people in your quiet town will recognize his face. The kind of things he did don't fall from your mind.'

'Monotony has changed. People have come and gone. Doubt anyone has lived here for more than five years.'

'There'll be someone.'

'I'll ask.' Cassidy tapped his chin and nodded. 'And even after fifteen years there'll be an outstanding arrest warrant. It might take some finding, but I'll track it down.'

'You won't find one.' Frank glanced back at Wayne, who hung his head. 'Because there ain't one.'

Cassidy narrowed his eyes. 'Three lawmen and a judge reckoned they knew who murdered a sheriff and they didn't fill out—'

'It was different in those days,' Frank roared, spit flying from his mouth. 'When I was a lawman we didn't get to sit around behind desks debating what to do. It was just us against scum like Wendell and we got on with the job and delivered justice.'

With the back of his hand Cassidy batted imaginary spit from his jacket. He leaned forward from his chair to glare back at Frank.

'And your incompetence in those days doesn't help me in these days.'

Frank glared back, but with a snap of his neck he hung his head.

'I'm sorry,' he muttered. 'But. . . .'

Cassidy glanced at the other men, who all looked away. He nodded.

'Perhaps it *was* different then. And as the investigation into Sheriff McAlister's death starts properly with me, I can tell you that with no warrant, no witnesses and no proof, Wendell Moon has nothing to answer to.'

Frank looked up. He sneered, slammed his palms down on the desk, and leaned forward, placing his face to within inches of Cassidy's.

'Then answer me this – are you calling four former lawmen liars?'

Cassidy contemplated Frank's firm gaze, then glanced away.

'I'll talk to Wendell.'

Frank pushed back from the desk and hitched his gunbelt higher.

'Good. We'll back you up.'

Cassidy lifted a hand. 'I have two deputies. I don't need help from you old-timers.'

'Old-timers! Have more respect before I—'

Jackson slammed a hand on Frank's shoulder.

'Enough, Frank,' he said. 'Let Cassidy do it his way. This is his town.'

'Yeah,' Frank muttered and kicked at the desk. 'But Ben McAlister wouldn't have spoken to an ex-lawman that way.'

Cassidy brushed past Frank and walked to the door.

'I ain't Ben McAlister,' he said.

CHAPTER 4

'How far to Monotony?' Zachary Forester asked the bartender.

'Fifty miles.' The bartender smiled. 'And that's an awful long way without a drink.'

Zachary nodded and licked his lips.

'You're right,' he said. 'Four whiskeys.'

'Coming right up.'

Zachary rolled back to glance around the trading post.

Customers lounged against the bar, considering their purchases. Drinkers filled the rough benches.

Zachary turned and grabbed his whiskey. He lifted it to his lips, but then put it down.

'Trails head south and east from here. I'm looking for someone. I reckon he's heading for Monotony, but he might have headed into Carmon.'

The bartender glanced at Zachary's three men and shrugged.

'Then head into Carmon. If he ain't there, he probably went south.'

Zachary ran the glass through his fingers. 'But I

reckon you could save me a journey.'

'Can't help.' The bartender strode down the bar.

'I ain't said what he looked like yet,' Zachary shouted after him.

The bartender stopped but kept his back to Zachary.

'And you ain't heard me. I can't help.'

'There were five men in all. The one I'm interested in would be grey haired by now.'

The bartender grunted his indifference and grabbed a towel from under the bar.

A portly man, Bill Matthews, strode to the bar. With his hands on his hips he squared off to Zachary.

'You heard the man,' he said. 'He can't help. So stop asking questions, drink your whiskey, and leave.'

Zachary glanced at Bill, appraising his pendulous belly. He shrugged and lifted the whiskey to his lips, then with a swirl of his arm threw it into Bill's face.

As Bill spluttered, Zachary slugged him low and hard. Bill doubled over clutching his guts.

Zachary followed through by thrusting up his knee to slam it into Bill's face.

Footsteps pounded behind him.

He spun round to face a flailing fist from another man. Zachary took a blow to the cheek that knocked him back against the bar. He shook his head, spat on his hand, and weighed in with a solid blow to his assailant's jaw that sent him sprawling.

A row of men stood from the benches and squared up to him.

'We don't like curious strangers,' the tallest man, Wolf Smith, said, flexing his fists. 'You'll learn what happens when you ask too many questions.'

With a short lunge, Zachary pulled his gun, each of his men matching the action.

'Reckon as you are too,' Zachary muttered.

Wolf lifted his hands, eyeing the row of guns pointing his way.

'Ain't no need for that.'

'Man has a right to defend himself.'

'He has.' Wolf lowered his hands a mite, drifting them down to his gunbelt.

'Stop,' a heavily-bearded man, Dave Bowman, shouted. He stood from his bench. 'I came here for a quiet drink. Ain't wanting gunfire all around.'

Wolf nodded. 'This man is speaking sense. Put your gun down, stranger, while you still can.'

Zachary shook his head. 'Not until I get some answers.'

'You'll get none here.'

Dave pushed through the row of men facing Zachary. When he was clear, he folded his arms and backed a pace so that he had everyone in view.

'He will. I just came from Monotony. A group of men rode into town as I left and another group was five miles back from the trading post. One of those was probably the group this man is looking for.'

Wolf snorted. 'You just earned a kicking out of here too.'

'That information won't hurt anyone.' Dave glanced at Zachary and chuckled. 'These scum couldn't harm any of those men. The nearest group had the look of lawmen. They were old but they could handle themselves. And as for the others, they had a short, podgy man and a well-heeled gentleman with grey hair, but the others were gunslingers.'

Zachary nodded. 'They sound like the men I'm looking for.'

'Hope they're friends of yours. They'd rip you in two without any effort.'

Zachary sneered, and with a last glare around the trading post he gestured to Lester. With their guns held at arm's length they backed to the door and outside.

Everyone returned to their benches. A few men glared at Dave, but then shrugged and hunched over their drinks.

When the room had returned to its previous quiet state a gangling youngster slipped to his feet from the back of the room. He wended through the customers and strode outside.

Nobody looked up to watch him leave.

Outside, he lifted his hand to his brow and watched the four men who'd left before him trot down the trail, heading for Monotony.

When they were out of sight beyond the first hill, he mounted his horse and trotted after them.

'According to Frank Taylor,' Cassidy said, 'you have some questions to answer.'

Wendell chuckled and leaned back in his saloon chair. He glanced at his gunslingers, who echoed his chuckle, then glanced at the portly man who had just joined him.

'This is Phillip Tannin,' Wendell said. 'He's my business partner, but he also deals with our legal matters. Usually that just involves contractual concerns, but he can represent me.'

Phillip extracted a handkerchief and mopped his sweating brow.

'And I'd advise Mr Moon not to answer your questions,' he said, his voice high-pitched.

'You don't know what the questions are yet,' Cassidy snapped.

'Mr Moon has appraised me of Mr Taylor's ill opinion of him and your presence suggests that you wish to continue his line of questioning. So my advice stands.'

'That's good advice,' Cassidy said. He glared down at Phillip. 'But I'd like to keep this a friendly chat in a saloon. So if you don't change your advice, we can discuss this in my office with your business partner sitting in a cell.'

'That is most—'

Wendell slammed a hand on Phillip's arm. 'No need to trouble our lawman. I have nothing to hide.' He looked up at Cassidy and smiled. 'Ask your questions, Sheriff, and I'll answer.'

Cassidy nodded and turned to Wendell.

'According to Frank you once killed a man.'

Wendell leaned back in his chair and considered Cassidy.

'Just a man. He's wrong.' Wendell lifted his hat to push back a wisp of his thinning hair. 'I've killed two men.'

Cassidy cocked his head to one side, his hand twitching a few inches towards his gunbelt.

'Oh?'

Wendell replaced his hat. 'I had some exploits when I was younger. To be honest I wasn't a nice person. I double-crossed a few men and received a few double-crosses in return. One of the men who double-crossed me was Clay Hilton.'

Wendell kicked out a spare chair and gestured to it.

Cassidy shook his head and settled his stance.

'Carry on.'

Wendell looped his boot round the chair and pulled it back. He lifted his foot on to it.

'Clay was even worse than I was then. If you tracked down anyone who knew him, I'm sure they'd want to congratulate me.'

'You saying you had good cause to kill him?'

'Yup. It's a long story and I'll tell you it if you want, but we're both busy men.' Wendell pulled a silver-plated fob watch from his waistcoat and glanced at it. He winced, then looked up at Cassidy. 'Is he the man you mean?'

'Nope.'

'I killed my second man after I left here.' Wendell swung his watch back and forth. 'I've forgotten his name, just as I've forgotten the hand he had.'

'You saying you had good cause for that killing too?'

'Nope. He beat me fairly with some fine poker playing, but I didn't like it. I lay in wait—'

'Wendell,' Phillip murmured. 'I must advise you to not volunteer this information.'

'As I said – I have nothing to hide.' Wendell glared at Phillip until he lowered his head, then turned back to Cassidy. 'I lay in wait, ambushed him, and took back everything I'd lost. Then I ran. Except Marshal Mortimer tracked me down. He treated me fairer than I expected. I thought I'd swing, but he chained me up and sent me to Leavenworth State Penitentiary to rot. I did twelve years.'

'Twelve years is a long time.'

Wendell rocked his foot from the chair and shuffled round to fix Cassidy with his firm, blank gaze.

'Yup. But it was time well spent. If I'd escaped from the marshal I'd have carried on living by my wits and I'd be long dead by now, but in jail I met a man with an idea about how to get rich.' Wendell glanced at Phillip and smiled. 'His idea involved being on the right side of the law and ahead of the railroads. When I left jail I headed west after him, and the rest is a different tale. And one of which any man can be proud.'

Wendell widened his smile, revealing two gold teeth.

Cassidy nodded, eyeing the silver-plated watch that Wendell dangled in his left hand.

'I ain't talking about that murder either. I'm talking about Sheriff Ben McAlister.'

With his right hand Wendell opened his waistcoat pocket and swung the watch in.

'I remember him. He ran me out of town. How did he die?'

Cassidy searched Wendell's face for any hints that he was feigning ignorance, but he sat impassive and relaxed, his blank eyes wide.

'Gang of outlaws ambushed him in his home

around the time you left Monotony.'

Wendell considered his hands. He shrugged.

'I wasn't involved.'

'Thought you'd say that, but I just wanted to hear the words. Can you prove it?'

Wendell glanced at Phillip, who leaned forward.

'Sheriff,' Phillip said, 'you do know that that ain't the way the law works, don't you? Nobody has to prove their innocence. The law must prove otherwise.'

'I know, but we ain't doing this officially.' Cassidy provided his most benign smile. 'We're just having a friendly chat in a saloon.'

Wendell looked up to meet Cassidy's gaze, nodding.

'When Sheriff McAlister ran me out of town,' he said, 'our outlaw band settled old scores, then broke up. Any one of a dozen men could have returned and killed him. For me, I just ran. Ain't proud of that, but more people had taken exception to me than supported me, so I just preserved my hide and rode as fast as I could.'

Cassidy lowered his head. 'I'd like to believe you.'

'Sheriff, only a stupid man would return to a town where he'd killed a lawman. I ain't stupid. But I am a rich and successful businessman.' Wendell sat back in his chair. 'I ain't saying I was a saint the last time I passed through. I did plenty of wrong, but twelve years is the price I paid for my former life.'

Cassidy nodded. 'And in your new life, you ain't looking for trouble?'

'Nope.'

Cassidy backed a pace and tipped back his hat.

'Then I'll see that trouble won't come your way. I'll tell Frank Taylor to give you leeway. You're in no danger.'

Wendell threw back his head to roar his laughter, exaggerating his mirth with a slap of his rounded belly.

'I ain't quaking in my boots.'

'You should be. Four men have a mighty strong belief that you have some questions to answer.'

With a slow lick of his lips, Wendell suppressed his laughter.

'The only people in danger are Frank and his decrepit friends. They're old-timers and I don't want them to die, but before, your arrival saved *their* lives, not mine.' He nodded to the men sitting opposite. 'These are my employees, Stark, Thorpe and Lance.'

The gunslingers grinned and tipped their hats.

'Howdy,' they said in unison.

'I used to live with a gun, but I live by the dollar now and that means I pay for the best protection. If any of those old-timers had moved for their guns, they'd be dead before they finished that move.'

Cassidy glanced at the gunslingers. 'I run a law-abiding town.'

'And you have the word of a law-abiding man that I won't look for trouble, but if Frank or any of those old-timers come looking for it, they'll find it.' Wendell leaned forward, a firm stare replacing his former jovial expression. 'If you want them to live, warn them away.'

*

'Wendell's admitted that he used to live on the wrong side of the law,' Cassidy said when he rejoined Stirling and the others outside the Palomino Hotel. 'But he served twelve years in Leavenworth jail and when he came out, he resolved to go straight. From the sound of it, he has.'

'He ain't changed,' Frank muttered. He slammed the flat of his hand against a post. 'Did he admit to everything he did in Monotony?'

'He volunteered plenty more than he had to, and I see no reason to suppose he killed Sheriff McAlister.'

Frank snorted. 'And how did you decide that? Did you just ask him if he did it?'

Cassidy folded his arms. 'I did.'

'And when he said "no", that satisfied you?'

'I saw no reason to believe he lied.'

Frank stalked around the post, shaking his head. When he reached Cassidy again he leaned back against the post and took long breaths.

'Wendell is the sneakiest, lowest snake I've known. Every word that man utters is a lie.' Frank gestured to Jackson and the others. 'But we don't lie. You can trust us. Wendell Moon killed Ben McAlister.'

'I do trust you, but you have no proof that he did it, and you'll have to do more than parade your conviction to convince me.'

Frank snorted. 'That man did enough to swing ten times. The Forester gang were the roughest I've known.'

Cassidy tipped back his hat. 'I ain't heard of the Forester gang, but people have told me about the

Smythe gang – and they *were* rough. Since I moved here, I've—'

Frank pushed back from the post and took a long pace towards Cassidy.

'What you trying to tell me?'

Cassidy drew himself up to his full height. 'I'm telling you that I've met and sorted plenty of rough varmints, and I judge that Wendell Moon is a law-abiding businessman.'

'If you'd stood in that house fifteen years ago and seen the bodies, you wouldn't say that.' Frank slammed his bunched fist into his other hand with a resounding slap. 'Time doesn't take that away.'

'I understand, and if I find proof that Wendell Moon killed Sheriff McAlister, I'll take him into custody. But this is a law-abiding town and your days of delivering summary, rough justice are over, so while I investigate, don't bother him.'

'We're lawmen,' Frank roared, his face reddening. 'You can't threaten us.'

'You ain't lawmen no more,' Cassidy snapped. He glared at Frank, then glanced away. He sighed and patted Frank's shoulder. 'But I ain't threatening my own kind. Just stay within the law and don't give Wendell's gunslingers an excuse to show us their skills. Then we'll get on fine.'

Frank flinched away from Cassidy's hand, his eyes blazing.

'Lock up Wendell and we will.'

Stirling grabbed Frank's arm and pulled him back.

'Sheriff,' Stirling said, 'Frank is trying to say that you won't get any trouble from us.'

Frank muttered under his breath, then swung away to stalk two paces down the boardwalk.

Cassidy shrugged. 'I'd explain that to Frank too.'

Stirling nodded. 'I will. But just take some advice from men who know Wendell Moon. Where he goes, trouble ain't far away. You won't keep this town law-abiding for long.'

Cassidy looked at each man in turn, lingering on Frank's back, but Frank kept his gaze set forward. With a shake of his head and a tip of his hat to Stirling, Cassidy sauntered back across the road to his office.

With his arms folded Stirling watched Cassidy saunter away, then turned to speak with Frank, but Frank was stalking into the Palomino Hotel, followed by Wayne and Jackson.

Stirling strode on to the boardwalk, but warmth tingled on the back of his neck. Keeping his movements steady, he glanced across the road.

Leaning against the bank wall, a long-coated man glared at him, his face too far away for Stirling's poor eyesight to discern the features. Then, seeing Stirling looking at him, he pushed from the wall and strode into the alley beside the bank.

With a half-remembered recollection narrowing his eyes, Stirling watched the man disappear into the alley's shadows.

Stirling shook himself and followed the others into the hotel.

CHAPTER 5

Zachary Forester dismounted and stood facing James Whittler's farmhouse. He glanced around the farm, then nodded to his men to dismount. Behind them the sun edged close to the low hills, casting their long shadows forward and etching their forms in sharp relief.

Using his thumb and forefinger Zachary raised his hat to the ruddy-faced farmer who strode from his farmhouse.

'You'll be James Whittler,' he said.

'Yup,' James said, squinting into the sun with a hand raised to his brow. 'And you must be Wendell Moon.'

Zachary gritted his teeth, his hands tightening.

'Nope. I work for him.'

'But he's still coming tomorrow, ain't he?'

A momentary smile broke Zachary's grim visage.

'Yeah. He's still coming tomorrow. We're just here to check facts so that Wendell is straight about everything.'

James nodded and folded his arms. 'What do you want to check?'

Zachary glanced at the farmhouse, then the barn. 'Are these the only buildings on your land?'

'Yup.'

By the barn a farmhand was lifting water from a well. Another farmhand was forking straw into the barn.

Zachary rubbed his chin. 'And how many people are on your land?'

James gestured back at the barn. 'Just me and my two boys.'

'No other farmhands, then? This is a big spread for just three men.'

'It is. That's why I'm glad to be selling.' James coughed, then kicked at the ground. 'Not that I'm keen on selling, you understand? If the price ain't what Wendell suggested, I ain't interested.'

Zachary lifted a hand. 'I'll be sure to let him know, but I just wanted to know how many people are on your land.'

'Just the three.'

Zachary licked his lips and glanced back at his men, receiving a row of eager grins.

'Just the three,' Zachary echoed, leaning forward to grin down at James.

James gulped and glanced at the men standing behind Zachary.

'Why are you so interested in that?'

'I wondered when you'd ask.' Zachary rolled his tongue along his bottom lip and spat to the side. His grin reappeared.

With a short lunge he pulled his gun and thundered lead into James's guts.

James staggered back and fell to his knees to receive a second shot through the neck.

Zachary spun round as lead blasted from each of his men. The air was thick with smoke as they blasted volley after volley at the two men by the barn. The dead men's prone bodies twitched with each gunshot.

'Enough,' Zachary shouted.

Silence returned to the farm. James and his two sons lay still in spreading pools of blood.

Zachary strode three paces and kicked James's lifeless body.

'Clear them away,' he muttered. 'And wash away the blood. I want this farm looking normal.'

'And then what?' Lester said, striding to Zachary's side.

'And then we wait.'

Deep into the evening, Frank Taylor leaned on the bar of the Lone Rider Saloon, a saloon situated at the opposite end of town to the Silver Streak. He ordered a whiskey, then nodded to the bartender to leave the bottle.

Stirling and the others had returned to their lodgings in the Palomino Hotel, conversation having been limited after sharing so many harsh words with the sheriff.

Frank turned to the old-timer at his side, who nursed an empty glass. He stared until the old-timer turned to him.

'Fancy a drink in that glass?' he asked.

The old-timer produced a huge, toothless grin and held out a shaking hand.

Frank filled the glass to the brim.

'Much obliged,' the old-timer said, his voice shaking and gritty. 'You just passin' through?'

'Don't aim to stay here long.' Frank swirled his whiskey glass. 'Things have changed around here recently.'

'Yup. Monotony's boomed, busted, and boomed some more.'

'Can't be many people around who've lived through all the booms and busts?'

'Nope.' With a shaking hand the old-timer poured a slug of whiskey into his mouth, a larger amount escaping to dribble down his chin. 'I reckon as I'm the only one who remembers Monotony when it was just two shacks 'side a trading post.'

'I reckon you can tell some tales about those days.'

'You reckoned right.'

Frank stared down into his whiskey glass. 'You remember the Forester gang?'

The old-timer scratched his head. He shrugged and swirled his whiskey.

'Remember the Smythe gang. Now there were some ornery devils. I can tell you tales about them that'll make the last of your hair go grey.'

'I ain't interested. I'd prefer to hear tales about the Forester gang.'

'Why?'

'Because of a man called Chase Longhorn.'

'That's me.' The old-timer flinched and shuffled

43

back a pace along the bar. 'How do you know me?'

Frank smiled. 'Chase Longhorn was a drunkard and a fighter. He broke Roy Foster's nose and drew a gun on his brother when he came looking for a return fight. Then he broke into . . . I could go on.'

'You know plenty.' The old-timer, Chase, leaned back on the bar. He knocked back his whiskey and sighed. 'In fact, you know more about me than I can remember these days.'

'Except you ain't recognized me yet.'

Chase threw up his hands, cringing, spraying the last of the whiskey on the floor.

'If I owe you money, I ain't—'

'You don't. I'm Frank Taylor, Sheriff Frank Taylor.' Frank hung his head and kicked the bar. 'Or at least I used to be.'

'Don't know you.'

'I arrived just after Sheriff Ben McAlister cleared out the Forester gang and I returned from time to time afterwards.'

Chase shrugged. 'And your problem with me?'

'Got none. I'd just like to hear what you remember about the Forester gang.'

Chase rubbed his forehead. He stared down into his empty glass and bared his toothless gums.

With a smile and a nod, Frank poured him a glassful.

Chase knocked back half his drink. 'Ain't rememberin' much, but from what I heard, they shot up a few things – not that there was much to shoot up in those days. Then they got to arguin' and headed west.'

44

'They *did* argue. But Ben McAlister ran them out of town.'

Chase shrugged. 'Maybe. I don't rightly remember.'

'I'd hoped you'd remember more.' Frank grabbed the whiskey bottle and swung away.

'If I thought me some more,' Chase shouted at Frank's back. 'I might remember somethin'. The whiskey loosens the mind.'

Frank turned. 'It does at that.'

Chase slapped a palsied hand against his forehead.

'Now that I think me some more – the Forester gang, yeah, I remember them. They shot up the town. And the sheriff he ain't happy and—'

'You don't remember.' Frank shuffled back. He chinked the bottle against Chase's glass, then placed the bottle on the bar inches from Chase's trembling right hand. 'But I bet you remember Wendell Moon.'

Chase nodded, a wide grin emerging. 'I surely do. He's that businessman who's buying land.'

'I don't mean from today,' Frank snapped. 'I mean from fifteen years ago. Wendell was in the Forester gang.'

'Doubt it. He's a right respectable businessman.'

Frank gritted his teeth. He considered Chase, then shook his head.

'Pity you don't remember.' He shook the whiskey bottle, then scraped it along the counter as he slipped it from Chase's lunging hand. 'This bottle is awful full.'

'Perhaps I ain't thinkin' straight,' Chase shouted. He licked his lips. A slow grin appeared. 'What d'you want me to remember?'

CHAPTER 6

Two hours after dawn Lester Jameson stood beside the window of James Whittler's farmhouse and peered outside. He dodged back from the window, smiling.

'Four horsemen are heading this way,' he said. Lester glanced out of the window. 'A tall man is in the centre. He's put on weight and he's stooped, but it's Wendell Moon.'

Zachary took a deep breath, enjoying the anticipation.

'Hope he's enjoying his last few minutes on earth.'

'His gunslingers are acting casual. I don't reckon they're expecting trouble out here. I reckon we can take them if you want Wendell alive.'

'Ain't worth the risk. I'll have everything I need when Wendell breathes his last.' Zachary rolled to his feet. 'Carl, Wendell's never seen you, so go outside and talk to them. Be real friendly but get them in here. Kent, welcome them in. Lester, keep your head down. I'll hide outside, then follow them in and Wendell will get a bullet in the back.'

Carl nodded and strode outside to meet the approaching riders.

With a last nod to Lester and Kent, Zachary slipped out the back door and to the corner of the house. He glanced around the side, confirming that he couldn't see the riders, then edged along the wall, stopping two paces from the front corner.

There, he listened.

'Howdy,' Carl hollered.

'Howdy to you,' Wendell said, leather creaking as he dismounted. 'You'll be James Whittler?'

As Zachary heard Wendell's voice for the first time in fifteen years, he crunched his fists so hard the knuckles cracked. He unflexed his hands and with care slipped his gun from its holster.

'I am,' Carl said. 'And I sure am glad you're here on this fine day. I reckon today will be profitable for both of us.'

'Me too. This here is a fine piece of land.'

'Glad you like it.'

'We've been around the perimeter this morning. Your estimate of the acreage sounds about right, so unless I find any problems, the price I offered is still available.'

'Even better news. Come in and we can finalize the details.'

'Not yet. I still have some things to see.'

Carl coughed. 'I have coffee on the stove.'

'Not interested. I want to see your spring and check on the well.'

At the side of the house, Zachary gritted his teeth.

'Get him in the house,' he whispered to himself.

'The spring,' Carl intoned, his voice low.

'Yeah. Water's important and you having a spring will solve plenty of problems. But it creates a few. I need to look at it.'

As Carl coughed and muttered to himself, Zachary's heartbeat thundered in his ears. Then Carl cleared his throat.

'I have a map in the house. We could look at that first.'

'No need. I have my own map.'

'Mine has plenty of details. We can enjoy that coffee while we examine it.'

'Mr Whittler,' Stark Masters said, interrupting, 'you seem mighty interested in getting us to go into your house.'

'I'm just being right friendly.'

Stark grunted.

'Get him in there,' Zachary whispered, sweat breaking out on his forehead. He wiped it away and edged a short pace nearer the corner of the house, his gun raised to his shoulder.

'I ain't got all day,' Wendell muttered. 'So you can be right friendly showing me around your land instead.'

'I really,' Carl muttered, raising his voice, 'want to show you something in the house.'

Wendell murmured low words. A hand slapped leather, a gunshot sounding a scant second later.

With a short oath, Zachary swung out from the house.

Twenty yards before the house Carl faced Wendell and his three gunslingers. Carl staggered back and around, his hands framing a spreading red bloom on his chest. Stark put a second bullet in his back before he hit the ground.

Zachary swung his gun round, arcing it towards Wendell, but a volley of gunshots from Stark peppered the side of the house. Splinters flew into Zachary's face.

In desperate self-preservation Zachary fell back without firing a single shot.

He edged back and forth, but he had to accept his exposed situation and the complete lack of cover nearby. With his head down he dashed back along the side of the house. He skidded around the back corner as another volley of gunshots blasted at his heels.

He dashed to the back door and charged inside.

'That idiot,' he roared.

'Wasn't Carl's fault,' Lester muttered from beside the front window. 'Wendell wasn't coming in here no matter what he said.'

Zachary gritted his teeth and dashed to the second window at the front of the house. He peered outside.

Wendell had fallen back. Lance and Thorpe had hunkered down beside a cart. Stark wasn't visible.

'We ain't getting Wendell easily now,' he muttered. He glanced at the back door. 'Kent, guard the back door. We'll hold them off at the front.'

Kent nodded and dashed to the back door. He reached it just as it slammed back against the wall so hard it fell to the floor.

Kent danced back to avoid the falling door, but Stark leapt through the doorway. In desperation

Kent grabbed him and pushed him back against the doorframe.

Zachary aimed his gun at them, but with no clear shot, he waited for an opening. Beside him Lester did the same as Kent and Stark struggled by the door.

Gunshots peppered through the window, slicing shards of glass in all directions.

Zachary swung round. Outside, Thorpe dashed to closer cover. Zachary fired off a shot, the blast slamming into the ground feet away from Thorpe.

A gunshot sounded inside the room and Kent fell away from Stark. With Stark standing alone Lester and Zachary charged him, aiming their guns towards him.

Stark hunched, blasted a bullet into Lester's guts, then swung his gun with lightning speed towards Zachary.

Zachary leapt to the floor, skidding on his shoulder as he aimed up at Stark. From such a hard position his shot blasted wide and, as he took better aim, Stark was upon him, kicking his gun arm. The gun arced away.

Zachary scrambled to his knees to receive a second polaxing kick to the chin. He lay stunned, waiting for the lead that would end his life but with no way to defend himself.

Seconds passed without the pain coming.

As his breath and vision returned he rolled to a sitting position. Stark stood over him, the gun pointing at his head, a huge grin and cold eyes framing the gun.

Behind, the door swung open and Thorpe and

Lance swaggered inside.

'He the last one?' Thorpe asked.

'Yup,' Stark said.

'Worst ambush I've ever seen. Who are these idiots?'

'Kept this one alive just so you could ask him.'

Thorpe strode across the room to glare down at Zachary.

'So, you're the man who was tracking Mr Moon. Why?'

'Mr Moon,' Zachary spat. 'He ain't no mister. He's just Wendell, a low-down, double-crossing varmint.'

'We already figured you ain't a friend of his. But answer the question.'

Zachary glanced around, covering his action by rubbing his chin and wincing.

From the corner of his eye he saw his gun lying beside the back door. It was ten feet away. He looked away and knelt, edging a foot closer to his gun.

'I'll answer that question. But I'll only answer to Wendell.'

'Tell me and Mr Moon will hear the answer.'

Zachary dropped his head to scratch the back of his neck. He shuffled round, edging back another foot.

'And when I give you the answer, what happens to me?'

Thorpe grinned. 'We let you go.'

Lance and Stark chuckled.

Zachary tipped back his hat and sighed. 'Thought as much.'

'Sooner you talk,' Thorpe said, lifting his gun

higher and widening his grin, 'the sooner you can be on your way.'

'I'll tell you outside. Always reckoned my last moments on earth should be spent outside and not cooped up inside.'

Thorpe nodded and gestured to the front door with his gun hand.

With the gun pointing to the door, Zachary leapt backwards. His long dive landed on his gun. He shuffled the gun into his hands and carried on the roll through the door.

Gunshots cannoned into the floor behind him, a ricochet ripping through trouser cloth.

Outside Zachary rolled to the side and scrambled to his feet. With his arms flailing for balance he dashed to the corner of the house. He skidded around the corner and pressed his back to the wall. With large gulps he regained his breath.

He glanced left and right; his head on one side as he listened for the footfalls the men would make when they emerged from the house.

He only heard the wind rustling around the house.

He glanced at the barn, judging that it was fifty yards away. This was the nearest cover. Zachary smiled.

Lester had stationed their horses in the barn.

One silent footstep at a time he edged back from the house, keeping himself mid-way from both corners.

Pace by pace the land around the house appeared – the cart, Carl's body before the house, the men's horses tethered to a fence. But he didn't see the gunslingers or Wendell.

Behind Zachary, the barn came closer and closer.

When he was halfway to the barn he debated whether he should search for Wendell or just survive for a second attempt.

He dashed for the barn.

Behind him somebody scrambled from the house and, feeling an itch on his back, he leapt to the ground, gunshots blasting over his tumbling form as he rolled through the barn door.

He scrambled to the side on hands and feet and pressed against the barn wall. He gathered his breath, then jumped to his feet and glanced around the barn.

The horses had gone.

He blinked hard and looked again, but only piles of hay faced him.

'Wendell,' he muttered to himself, logging another reason why Wendell would pay for his treachery.

He edged back to the barn door and glanced outside. Stark stood outside the house. Thorpe and Lance were edging to the side to take positions behind the cart.

'You looking for something in there?' Stark shouted.

Zachary sorted through various oaths to scream back, then gritted his teeth and bottled his anger. He searched for a gap in the log wall and found a knot-hole. Through it he watched the gunslingers talk amongst themselves until Thorpe edged forward two paces.

'You're trapped in there,' Thorpe shouted.

'I prefer to think I have good cover,' Zachary shouted. 'You won't take me now.'

'We ain't in a hurry. You'll have to come out. We can wait.'

Zachary chuckled to himself. He liked taunting with the opposite of his intentions, and he guessed they did too.

For another minute he watched. Then a flurry of dust funnelled up behind the fence that arced round to the barn – Lance was crawling in a long circle to the barn to take him.

Zachary backed from the wall, searching for the most surprising place he could be hiding when Lance stormed in.

A ladder led to a second floor coated in piles of hay. He edged back to the door.

'I can wait too,' he shouted, then tiptoed to the ladder.

Just as he slipped a foot on the ladder a huge volley of gunshots sounded outside, followed by a second.

Zachary glanced up and judged that he didn't have enough time to clamber to the second floor.

He spun round. With his back pressed to the ladder, he kept the barn's front and back doors in view, waiting for the assault.

A rider hurtled through the front door. This man had his hat pulled low. Gunshots echoed behind him.

Zachary aimed his gun at the rider, but the rider fired over his shoulder, aiming outside, then pulled his horse to a shuddering halt. He held out a hand.

'Get up here,' he shouted.

Zachary lowered his gun and charged for the horse. He grabbed the rider's offered hand and together they swung him on to the horse.

The rider shook the reins and they bolted for the barn's back door to emerge into the sunlight at a gallop. Zachary looked to the side.

The gunslingers were scurrying behind the cart while yelling at each other and gesticulating in all directions, seeming as bemused as Zachary was by this sudden appearance.

Zachary fired off a speculative shot but he judged that he was too far away and so concentrated on keeping still and letting his rescuer escape.

The rider vaulted the fence. Then they were on the open trail.

Two hundred yards from the farm Zachary glanced back but the pursuit still hadn't started.

'Got to thank you,' Zachary shouted. 'Whoever you are.'

'It can wait,' the rider said.

Zachary nodded. For the first time he realized just how young his rescuer's voice was.

CHAPTER 7

Sheriff Cassidy Yates looked up and down Monotony's main drag. Carts trundled past as the morning's business began, but he'd seen one of the men for whom he was searching.

He hitched his jacket closed and strode across the road to join Stirling Fontana on the boardwalk outside the Palomino Hotel. He nodded to him and leaned against a supporting post with a leg raised and his foot placed flat against the post.

'Just so you know, Stirling,' Cassidy muttered, 'I'm a real lawman. I ain't like you used to be.'

'What's that mean?' Stirling said, keeping his gaze on the road.

'It means I ain't stupid. Chase Longhorn came to see me last night for the first time without me going looking for him and he was full of whiskey and full of stories.'

Stirling shrugged. 'I ain't heard of a Chase Longhorn.'

'Chase is an old-timer – just like you. Except he's lived in Monotony longer than most and caused more trouble than most.'

Stirling turned to Cassidy, his eyebrows raised.

'That means he might remember Wendell Moon.'

'Really?' Cassidy chuckled. 'Well you're right. He does. And he told me a surprisingly lucid tale about Wendell's exploits fifteen years ago.'

Stirling nodded. 'Told you somebody in town would remember what Wendell Moon did.'

'Yeah, but his tale was similar to the one Frank told me.'

Stirling narrowed his eyes.

'It would be,' he said, his voice guarded, 'as the tale Frank told you was the truth.'

'Except his tale was so similar, it makes me wonder what to believe.'

Stirling sighed and glanced away. 'Still don't get your meaning.'

Cassidy pushed from the post and strode round to stare at Stirling.

'Then I'll put it plainer. I'm watching you and your fellow *ex*-lawmen more than I'm watching Wendell Moon and his gunslingers. You continue being this stupid, I'll run you out of town – ex-lawmen or no ex-lawmen.'

Stirling opened his mouth to complain, then hung his head.

Cassidy glared at Stirling's downturned head, then turned on his heel.

Stirling looked up to watch the sheriff stride back to his office.

'Frank,' he muttered under his breath. 'You idiot.'

*

On the edge of a forest, five miles from James Whittler's farm, Zachary and his rescuer stopped.

Zachary swung down from the horse and waited for the other man to do the same.

'I'm obliged to you . . .' Zachary tipped back his hat, '. . . boy.'

The dark-haired youngster shrugged his jacket around his bony frame and sneered.

'I ain't a boy.'

Zachary nodded. 'Guess you ain't. You did a man's job back there.'

'Glad to hear it, Mr Forester. Or seeing as how I rescued you, I reckon I can call you Zachary.'

'You know plenty about me. If you don't want me to keep calling you "boy", you'll pay me the courtesy of your name.'

'I'm Henry, Henry Fontana.' Henry searched for any hint of recognition in Zachary's cold eyes, but Zachary just nodded.

'Well met, Henry Fontana. Now why do you know me?'

Henry chuckled and a huge grin broke out.

'Everyone knows about Wendell Moon and Zachary Forester.'

Zachary kicked a stone and looked to the horizon. He sighed.

'Not any more they don't.'

'I don't reckon that's right.' Henry whistled through his teeth. 'I just can't believe it. Zachary Forester is right here before me. Is it true that you once faced up to Marshal Devine?'

With a rueful smile Zachary rubbed an old scar on his cheek.

'Yeah. One of my many mistakes, but you didn't rescue me to ask about old exploits.'

'I didn't. I've been tracking you for days. I reckoned that where you went, Wendell Moon wouldn't be far away. Seems I was right.'

'Why did you reckon that?'

Henry stood back, his eyes glazing.

'The Forester gang,' he said, his level tone sounding as if he was reading, 'was the first and most famous outlaw gang to terrorize Monotony. The law couldn't stop them.'

Zachary couldn't stop jutting his chin. 'You're right there.'

'But then it fell apart when Wendell turned on the gang's leader. . . .' Henry coughed and glanced at Zachary. 'That'd be you. He killed Clay Hilton and would have killed you too but you hightailed it out of town.'

Zachary narrowed his eyes. 'You know a lot about those days.'

'My pa told me tales.'

Zachary nodded. 'Did I know him?'

'Nope.' Henry glanced away. 'He wasn't on your side of the law.'

'So if your pa was a lawman, why are you here?'

Henry puffed his slight chest. 'I'm my own man. I make my own decisions and I look for my own truths. So here I am, looking for the truth about what happened between you and Wendell.'

'The truth's only lies and acts that shouldn't interest a decent boy like you.' Zachary turned to stare
away, sneering.

Henry gulped. 'You're right, but for now, I only
care about Wendell.'

'Then follow the lawmen. They're the only ones
with a chance of getting him now.'

'I don't reckon so – not when the two of us are
together.'

Zachary snorted. 'We ain't together. I ain't siding
with some scabby-kneed, snot-nosed kid.'

Henry bunched his small fists, then abated his
anger with a slow count to five.

'I ain't a—'

'Just think yourself lucky that I didn't kill you.'
Zachary stormed towards Henry's horse. 'We're
through.'

'You will side with me,' Henry shouted. 'You have
no choice.'

Zachary slid to a halt. He turned, smiling
ruefully.

'Sadly, you're probably right. But why would a fine,
upstanding son of a lawman want to join an old
outlaw just to get another old outlaw?'

'Lawmen are just doing their job, but when a man
gives his word and goes against it, he deserves to die.'

Zachary glanced away, rubbing his chin, then
turned back to Henry.

'You got it right there.'

'Yup. And I know plenty more. I'll be useful in
getting Wendell.' Henry provided a youthful grin.

Zachary sighed. He closed his eyes a moment.

'Can't believe I'm doing this.' He held out a grimed hand. 'But put it there, partner.'

Deep into the afternoon, four men stood beside two moss-coated rock piles. Behind them the cemetery stretched down the hillside.

In the last fifteen years the cemetery had sprawled in all directions, large headstones with full details replacing the simple wooden crosses or scrawled notes trapped beneath rocks of their day.

Such were the changes that they'd taken an hour to locate these rocks.

Frank shook his head. 'I ain't sure this is it. I reckon we buried them beside an oak.'

'This is it,' Stirling muttered. 'I'll never forget this spot.'

He knelt beside the cairns and scraped away the mulch of last year's leaves. He found neither flowers nor the flat rock into which he'd scraped an inscription.

He bowed his head and whispered low words.

The others didn't hear but they knew the sentiment.

Frank grunted. 'Come on. We have a promise to keep.'

Frank turned and Jackson and Wayne followed, but Stirling stared down at the cairns. He glanced back, noting that they were giving him a moment.

'I ain't sure if this is really you, Ben, but I just thought you ought to know.' Stirling coughed and cleared a throat that felt smaller than it should be. 'My eldest boy's becoming a fine man, just as your boy would have. He's a bit headstrong, but you'd be proud of. . . .'

A pang of doubt hit him as to whether this really was Ben's grave and, feeling foolish at talking to a rock pile, he turned and strode after the others.

Chase Longhorn staggered from the saloon. With sunset some hours back, he'd already drank away half of the money that Frank Taylor had given him, but that still left another day, perhaps two, of whiskey, before he'd need to revert to his usual tricks.

With his gait rolling, he wandered off the edge of the boardwalk. He stumbled to his knees and swayed, then staggered to his feet. He aimed for the edge of town, pointed, then snaked down the road.

'Chase,' a man said.

'Yeah,' Chase murmured. He staggered in a circle, glancing around.

In the dark, the nearby people hurried by him, the oil-lamps and fires either silhouetting their forms or transfixing them in harsh detail. Nobody was looking at him.

Chase shrugged. He pointed in the direction he wanted to go and set off again.

'Chase.'

This time, Chase had caught the direction of the voice. He spun on his heel, swayed, and stood. He stared down the darkened alley beside the Silver Streak Saloon.

In the shadows a lone man stood, only his outline visible.

'What you want?' Chase slurred.

The man backed into the shadows.

Chase shrugged his trousers higher and rubbed his forehead. But with his curiosity peaked and the thought that this might be Frank offering to give him more whiskey money, he staggered down the alley. Within, the darkness encased him, the sounds from the road now muffled and distant.

With his hands out in case he walked into anything, he staggered further down the alley.

A shape loomed close.

Chase flinched and stopped. 'Who's that?'

The shape loomed closer. Bright eyes and a smile reflected light.

'You want me?' Chase said.

Another reflection appeared, this time of gunmetal.

Chase gulped.

Light flashed and hot pain thundered into his guts. Warm stickiness flowed over his hands as he grasped his chest.

Two more blasts ripped through him and the darkness closed in.

CHAPTER 8

'Is it Chase Longhorn?' Sheriff Cassidy Yates asked as Deputy Giles emerged from the alley.

'How did you know?' Giles asked, raising his hand to block the low, early-morning sun.

Cassidy tipped back his hat. 'When Deputy Hearst said you'd found a body, I just somehow knew.'

'Someone shot him three times.' Giles pointed at his guts. 'Can't say I ain't surprised that someone's had enough of Chase. It'll be tough working out who did it.'

Cassidy chuckled. 'Guess you could start by rounding up half the town.'

'I could. Chase made enough enemies.' Giles glanced back at the Palomino Hotel – Stirling Fontana was striding towards them. 'But it's strange that he died just after some argumentative newcomers arrived in town. And one of those newcomers seems to have found out quickly what happened.'

'Stirling coming here just saves me a journey.' Cassidy hitched his jacket closed and strode into the road.

*

After his discussion with the sheriff, Stirling stormed into the Palomino Hotel and with his knees creaking with the extra effort, he took the steps three at a time. He strode straight to Frank's room. Without knocking he kicked the door open to find Frank staring out of the window.

'Frank,' he muttered. 'We need to talk.'

Frank turned, sneering, then forced a grim smile.

'I'm listening.'

'Chase Longhorn is dead.'

Frank raised his eyebrows. 'I shouldn't gloat, but Chase was a worthless varmint when I first met him and I doubt he improved much.'

Stirling grabbed the open door and slammed it shut.

'Why would you gloat?'

'We were right. Before too much longer Wendell would return to his old tricks. That sheriff may have been doing his duty in protecting him, but he'll also do his duty and arrest him now.'

Stirling paced across the room to the window. He stared down at the road where Deputy Giles was directing a black-coated undertaker into the alley by the saloon.

'He ain't doing that.'

'He has to. Wendell – or at least one of his gunslingers – killed Chase.' Frank pointed at the Coronet Hotel, where Sheriff Cassidy Yates was striding through the door. 'I bet he's gone to arrest Wendell now.'

66

'He ain't. If he's gone into the hotel to see Wendell, it's to tell him that he has nothing to fear.'

'What?' Frank shouted, turning from the window.

'Cassidy knows you bribed Chase to tell him about Wendell, so he also suspects that such a lawman might also frame Wendell for murder.'

'He can't prove anything.' Frank hung his head and threw up his hands to place them on either side of the window. He leaned his weight forward. 'And you? Do you support Cassidy?'

'I don't know. I'd like to think you wouldn't, but I know your old techniques. You. . . .' Stirling sighed. 'I don't reckon you'd kill an innocent man to get Wendell, but you'd do most more besides.'

'Obliged.' Frank pushed back from the window and turned away. He sighed long and hard. 'But you're right. I did kill Chase.'

'Frank.'

While still looking away from Stirling, Frank lifted a hand.

'I didn't pull the trigger but it was my fault.'

'You mean you forced Chase out into the open and once Wendell knew a potential witness was still alive, he had to dispose of him?'

'Yeah, but it's worse. Chase was the eldest resident I could find, but he arrived two years after Wendell killed Ben – just his mind was so drowned in whiskey, he couldn't remember.'

Stirling flopped down on to the windowsill.

'Then why did Wendell kill him?'

Frank turned. 'Perhaps he can't remember either, but he had to be sure.'

'From now on,' Stirling muttered, waggling a finger, 'no more tricks. Cassidy won't believe anything we say now, so we do this the right way. Stay out of trouble and let Wendell make the mistakes. Then we'll get him.'

Frank snorted and returned to staring through the window.

'Most unfortunate,' the plump attorney, Phillip Tannin, muttered as he bustled into the reception room of the Coronet Hotel.

Cassidy sighed. The previous day had been a continuous catalogue of failure. He hadn't found anybody who genuinely remembered Sheriff McAlister or Wendell Moon, and his trip to the sheriff's derelict house had uncovered nothing. The lack of even a starting place to his investigation had forced him to accept that his inquiry into the murdered lawman would end only hours after it had begun.

Now today had already started with a dead body and a pointless argument with Stirling Fontana, and he could see that the day was about to take another downturn.

'I'd prefer to discuss this unfortunate matter with your business partner,' Cassidy said.

Phillip glanced at the people sitting around the reception room, some were reading newspapers, but most were chatting. It'd only been ten minutes since the discovery of Chase's body, but wild rumours and gory details had already suitably enlivened the well-known facts.

Phillip took Cassidy's arm and led him across the reception room to a corner away from any interested people.

'Mr Moon is considering important business,' he said. 'I cannot disturb him, and especially not for every unfortunate matter that occurs.'

'Unfortunate ain't the word I'd use to describe murder.'

Phillip lowered his head a moment. 'Point taken, but that has nothing to do with Mr Moon.'

'Chase Longhorn is probably the only person who remembered Wendell from his last visit to Monotony.' Cassidy glared at Phillip until the plump man glanced away. 'And that is suspicious.'

'Perhaps, but Mr Moon has been involved in business all morning and I must be getting back to it.'

Phillip turned, but Cassidy grabbed his arm and spun him back.

'Mr Tannin, I was interested in what Mr Moon was doing last night.'

'He has no reason to answer that,' Phillip snapped. He rubbed the bridge of his nose, then sighed. 'But we are law-abiding men with nothing to hide. Yesterday Mr Moon was out of town on business. He didn't return until late. He went straight to this hotel and that is it.'

Cassidy lifted his hand. 'I'll check on that story.'

'You do that, but Mr Moon has nothing to hide and has no reason to want Chase Longfellow dead. If anyone should answer questions, Mr Taylor and those other men who bear a grudge against Mr Moon should answer them.'

'Chase Longhorn,' Cassidy murmured. He tipped his hat and glared through the window at the Palomino Hotel. 'But you don't need to explain my job to me. I'm already dealing with them.'

CHAPTER 9

The night was chill. With dawn three hours away the autumn stars and moon shone brightly through the windows of the Palomino Hotel as Frank Taylor tiptoed down the stairs, across the reception room, and on through the door.

On the deserted road the only movements came from a trio of horses bustling outside the Silver Streak Saloon.

Frank pulled his hat low and paced across the road to the Coronet Hotel.

None of the rooms had lights inside, their windows dead eyes in the night. Frank edged to the door and peered through.

The receptionist lay slumped over the desk, cradling his head on his arms.

Frank inched the door open, stopping at every squeak until he had a sizeable gap. He edged through the gap, then closed the door with the same care. He slipped across the reception room, keeping his gaze on both the receptionist and his route to the stairs.

A loud creak sounded.

With a foot raised Frank halted.

The receptionist grumbled in his sleep, then returned to his slumbers.

Frank judged that creeping across the room was more likely to attract interest than normal walking. Now with a firm stride he paced to the stairs and up two flights.

On the third floor he resumed his stealth, rolling his weight forward with every step down the hall.

Wendell's room was at the end of the corridor. Two doors back from it he stopped and slipped his gun from its holster. He resumed his steady pacing. At the door he halted.

For long minutes he listened to his own shallow breathing and the occasional night sounds of snoring and creaking from the cooling building.

He edged his hand to the doorknob. Just as his fingertips touched the knob, a dull scrape sounded from within the room.

Frank strained his hearing for another sound.

Long minutes passed without further noise. Frank gripped the knob and turned it a fraction.

Another scrape sounded from inside.

Frank nodded to himself.

Moving with extreme slowness he swung to the side, still gripping the doorknob, until he pressed his back against the wall. With his left arm outstretched he turned the knob.

The knob clicked from its catch.

Frank edged the door open a fraction.

Gunshots peppered the door from inside, their

sound destroying the night's peace, the door crashing shut with the force. Volley after volley blasted into the door and doorframe, splinters spraying the corridor.

Frank pressed back against the wall.

From other rooms cries went up.

'What's that?'

'Stay in!'

'What's happening?'

Frank kept his breathing shallow.

The door edged open and a gun slipped through the door followed by an arm.

Frank waited until the elbow appeared, then slammed his hand down on it, yanking the owner, Lance, out into the corridor. He slugged Lance to the jaw, knocking him back against the opposite wall for him to slide, unconscious to the floor.

He pressed back against the wall.

From inside the room Wendell clearly gave an order and another voice muttered something back.

From other rooms more voices sounded and from further down the corridor light drove away the darkness as somebody walked a lamp up the stairs.

Frank judged the merits of bursting into Wendell's room against retreating and saving his ambush for another day.

With a sigh, he backed from the door. He edged back along the corridor, speeding with each pace.

Hard steel jabbed into his back.

'I ain't causing this trouble,' he whispered. 'I was just investigating the gunfire.'

'Of course you are,' Thorpe muttered.

Frank snorted, then winced when Thorpe pressed the gun deeper into his back.

Thorpe pried the gun from Frank's grip and pushed him forward.

Frank staggered a pace, then walked down the corridor with his hands above his shoulders. At Wendell's room he stopped and glanced back at Thorpe.

'I have him,' Thorpe said and kicked Frank into the doorway.

Inside the room, Stark stood before Wendell, his gun trained on the doorway.

Stark smiled. 'We were expecting you.'

'You weren't. You just got lucky this time.'

Thorpe kicked Frank forward for him to stumble into the room.

'I don't believe in luck and Mr Moon didn't hire us to rely on luck either.'

Wendell gestured to Thorpe, who frisked Frank, then stood back. Wendell stood before Frank and looked him up and down, his blank eyes shining. He lit a cigar, puffed it, and blew out a circle of smoke.

'What you just tried to do ain't fitting for a lawman – even an ex-lawman who's too old to think straight.'

'Only thing that ain't fitting is that I failed.'

'You're too old for this, old-timer. It's time to rest and let the real lawmen deal with these matters.'

Frank snorted. 'I'm here because the real lawman in Monotony can't see through you. But I know the kind of man you are.'

'You know the kind of man I *was*. Cassidy Yates is a

real lawman and he worries about the kind of man I am now.'

'This ain't over, Wendell. We'll get you.'

Wendell grinned. 'You won't. From what I've seen – Wayne's too old, Jackson ain't got the guts and Stirling's too sensible.'

'Still leaves me.'

'It doesn't.' Wendell glanced at Thorpe, who raised his gun higher.

Frank lifted his chin and stared deep into Wendell's blank eyes.

'You wouldn't kill an unarmed man. The old you would, but now you're pretending to be a respectable businessman.'

Wendell tapped cigar ash on the floor and held his arms wide.

'A man has a right to defend himself and you've broken into my room.'

Frank stared into Wendell's eyes, judging if he would give the order. He lowered his head.

Without warning he leapt at Wendell and bundled him to the floor. He wrapped both hands around his neck and squeezed in a death grip that nothing could halt.

Somebody shouted an order behind him, but he didn't hear the words. Hands slammed on his back but he shrugged them off as he squeezed and squeezed Wendell's neck. His biceps creaked and his knuckles cracked as he tried to tighten his hands into one giant fist.

Wendell's eyes bulged. His mouth ripped open, clawing for air.

Frank squeezed, his bunched jaw muscles aching as he poured fifteen years of festering anger into his grip.

Below him, Wendell's face darkened.

Then, from behind, hot fire blasted into Frank's guts.

Still he squeezed.

But the strength oozed from his hands and his grip slackened despite his renewed effort.

Under his weak grip, Wendell wheezed in great gasps of air but Frank was slipping into a welcoming darkness.

CHAPTER 10

'Did he get him?'

Outside the Palomino Hotel Cassidy winced and glared at Stirling and Jackson.

'Is that all you can ask?'

Jackson shrugged. 'Yeah. It's the reason we came here.'

Cassidy glanced back at Wayne and Jackson who both nodded.

'You're all as bad as each other.' Cassidy sighed. 'But to answer your question – no. Wendell has some bruising and he'll be hoarse for a while, but he'll be fine.'

'Ain't saying I'm sad.'

Cassidy walked in a slow circle. On the opposite side of the road a crowd had gathered, many in their night clothes with coats wrapped against the chill, their conversation animated in the middle of the night.

Cassidy stopped his walk and jabbed a finger at Jackson's chest.

'This stops now. You're good men. You've done

more for this state than most, but I can't have this sort of behaviour.'

'You running us out of town?'

'Nope, but if I have to, I will.' Cassidy tipped back his hat. 'Don't make me.'

'We won't cause you trouble. But I assume you'll be making arrests.'

'What for?' Cassidy shouted, throwing up his hands. 'Frank broke into Wendell's room and tried to kill him.'

'Frank and Wendell just got to fighting and that ain't an excuse for his gunslingers to kill him.'

'They didn't kill Frank.' Cassidy took a pace forward and lifted on his heels as he stared down at Jackson. 'I did.'

'*You what?*' Jackson roared, pacing a long step towards Cassidy to stand toe to toe.

Cassidy held his ground. He placed his hands on his hips and glared deep into Jackson's eyes.

'I don't have to answer to you, but to make you end this madness, I'll tell you what happened. I heard shooting and went to the hotel. When I reached Wendell's room Frank had his hands around Wendell's neck. I tried to remove him but he wouldn't release his grip, so the only way to stop him killing Wendell was to shoot him.'

'You killed an old lawman to save a murderous varmint like Wendell Moon.' Jackson looked Cassidy up and down. He sneered and spat on the ground before Cassidy's boots. 'You ain't any kind of lawman I recognize.'

'And for that I'm grateful.' Cassidy tipped his hat

and turned. He stood with his back turned to Jackson. 'And if you try what Frank tried, I'll do the same to you.'

Lurking in the shadows, down by the Silver Streak Saloon, Zachary Forester watched Sheriff Yates talk with Stirling and Jackson. Henry stood at his side.

'What you reckon they're talking about?' Henry asked.

'Quit talking and watch,' Zachary snapped. 'Something's happened.'

Across the road Jackson advanced a long pace. He grabbed the sheriff's shoulder and spun him back to face him. He muttered low words close to Cassidy's face, then released his grip.

Cassidy waggled a finger in Jackson's face, then glared until Jackson stormed into the Palomino Hotel. Stirling and Cassidy shared a long stare, then Stirling turned, but instead of heading back into the hotel, he strode towards the closed saloon and straight at Zachary and Henry.

Keeping his movements casual, Zachary pushed back from the wall and sauntered down the board-walk.

Henry had disappeared but he didn't look back to search for him. He sauntered into the alley at the side of the saloon.

Down the alley, Henry cowered in the shadows with his back against the wall.

Zachary joined him and stared down the alley to the road, his hand resting on his gunbelt. Ten seconds later, Stirling strode past the alley, his head down and his hands in his pockets.

Zachary glanced round the corner to check that Stirling continued to pace down the road, then edged back into the alley. He chuckled.

'I have plenty of reasons for avoiding that ex-lawman,' Zachary said, 'assuming his memory is still intact, but I ain't sure why you're hiding.'

Henry shivered. 'A man who helps an outlaw has plenty of reasons to hide from a lawman, even an ex-lawman. Just reckon it's for the best if I keep out of his way.'

'No. That ain't it.' Zachary grabbed Henry's chin and, with his grimy fingers digging into his cheeks, he rocked his head from side to side. 'You already in trouble, boy?'

'Not yet,' Henry grunted through his distorted mouth. 'But I have run away from home and people might be looking to fetch me back.'

Zachary snorted. 'That ain't it either.'

Henry squirmed from Zachary's grip and rubbed his cheeks.

'Believe what you want.'

Zachary tapped his chin. He nodded. 'I remember now. The name of that old lawman is Stirling Fontana. He your relation, Henry?'

Henry glared back, his eyes bright in the night. Then he nodded.

'He's my pa.'

'Then why are you here?' Zachary snapped, looming over Henry. 'And this time, I want the real reason or my latest partner will be shortest lived of them all.'

Henry looked up and gulped. He backed up, his

head banging into the wall behind him. He rubbed his head and knocked his hat to the ground. With an embarrassed lunge he rummaged for his hat, but Zachary had slammed a firm foot on it.

Henry stood and faced up to Zachary.

'Pa wouldn't let me join in his quest to get Wendell. He said I had to stay behind and look after the farm.'

'Your pa speaks plenty of sense. This has nothing to do with you.'

'It has.'

Zachary edged his hand down to his gunbelt.

'You'll tell me why.'

Henry glanced at Zachary's hand, then lowered his head.

'Because my pa's too old for this.' Henry slammed his fist into his other palm. 'And with his gunslingers protecting him, Wendell will kill him and the other ex-lawmen. The only way I can save him is to do this myself.'

Zachary nodded. He removed his hand from his gunbelt and bent to pick up Henry's hat. He batted dust from it and handed it back to Henry.

'I ain't in a position to know if you're being stupid or brave, but it sounds to me like you got a mighty powerful reason to want Wendell Moon dead for yourself. But your pa won't like you siding with an outlaw.'

'The only thing that matters is that he comes out of this alive.' Henry swung the hat back on his head. 'But I reckon that when I tell him the truth, with time he'll believe me.'

Zachary narrowed his eyes. 'And the truth is?'

Henry stared back at Zachary, his lips pursed. He squared up to the larger man and jutted his chin.

'You'll either kill me or you won't, but the truth is – I didn't aim to save you. I'd followed you for days, wanting to see you finish Wendell so I'd know pa would be safe. When the shooting started, I thought you'd finish it. I rode to the farm to check, but I realized that you were in trouble and that Wendell would escape. A sort of red mist came down and I headed for the farm, but I panicked and veered off to the barn instead. I saved you but I didn't intend to.'

'You're an honest man. I don't meet many of them.' Zachary chuckled, then let it build into a full laugh. 'Guess as I don't care what your motives were at that farm. It's what you did that matters.'

'So now I've told you, I reckon you'll still be grateful enough to repay my act and help me.'

Zachary laughed louder. 'You what? You want *me* to help *you?*'

'Yup.'

Zachary licked his lips, suppressing his laughter. He kicked at the earth and glanced down the alley, then turned back to Henry.

'So then, Henry,' he said, his voice low but still amused, 'how can I help you get Wendell?'

'You've been going about it the wrong way.' Henry took a deep breath. 'My pa and his ex-lawmen's methods have about as much chance as yours did. He only knows the old ways and they don't work now. You can't just ride into town, call someone into the road, and kill them. Your plan to

82

ambush him was better, but Wendell was still prepared for it.'

'That's why I'm watching and waiting for another chance.'

'Still won't work. If you want to get Wendell, you need to outsmart him.'

'And you have a way of outsmarting him?'

Henry grinned. 'I sure do.'

Sitting in a high-backed chair in his room, Wendell patted his fingertips together as he contemplated Stirling. With a short wave, he ordered Lance to guard the door.

'I'm surprised you've waited this long to see me again,' he said, his voice gruff. 'Does Sheriff Yates know you're here?'

Stirling winced. Through the long, cold hours of the previous night he'd debated what to do after Frank's death. And just when he'd decided that seeing Wendell was the worst thing he could do, he'd done it anyhow.

He glanced around Wendell's opulent hotel room. The early morning sunshine glittered off the brass fittings and ornaments that adorned the wall-to-wall furniture – clearly Wendell had chosen the best room in Monotony.

He sneered. 'Nope.'

'From what I hear, Cassidy is close to running you out of town.' Wendell fingered the bandanna around his neck. 'One word from me—'

Stirling lifted a hand. 'That won't matter. It won't change your fate. There are other towns and other days. We've waited fifteen years. We can wait a while longer.'

Wendell shrugged. 'That mean you're leaving?'

'It might.' Stirling strode in a short circle. 'That depends on you.'

Wendell leaned further back in his chair. With an audible sigh he breathed through his nose, then nodded.

'Go on.'

'You're a conniving, devious wretch, Wendell, but before I decide whether we're leaving, I'm giving you a chance to tell me the truth about what happened fifteen years ago.'

'I double-crossed Zachary Forester. Sheriff McAlister ran me out of town. You know that.'

Stirling lowered his voice. 'You know what I mean. Did you kill Ben McAlister?'

Wendell chuckled. 'You've thirsted for revenge for fifteen years and only now are you asking that.'

'Now is the only time I'm interested in hearing your story. Sheriff Yates says you've paid for your crimes and you're a changed man. If that's so, you deserve a chance to explain yourself.'

Wendell ran a finger around his bandanna, loosening it a mite to reveal the deep fingertip bruises on his neck.

'And if I say I killed him, you'll just forgive me and walk away?'

'Nope,' Stirling snarled. 'It's like I said. Sheriff Yates believes you're just a businessman, but I know you. You're the lowest snake in hell. Nothing will stop me ending your worthless existence. But I just want to hear the truth.'

Wendell smiled and patted his fingertips together.

'And if I tell you, will you consider that as proof and take it to the sheriff?'

Stirling snorted. 'I wish I could, but my credibility with him is low. You could confess anything to me and he wouldn't believe me when I told him.'

'You're right. It's a fine thing when lawmen believe the word of ex-outlaws over the word of ex-lawmen.'

'It ain't,' Stirling snapped. 'And as I hate listening to you, quit crowing. What happened fifteen years ago?'

Wendell gestured to Lance who edged back, then glanced around the door into the hall to confirm nobody was outside. Lance swung back, closed the door, and nodded.

Wendell gestured to the table and scraped back a chair with his foot.

Stirling glared at the chair, then sat.

With a dart of his tongue Wendell licked his lips. He stared at his fingers as he tapped them together, then looked up and stared into Stirling's eyes, his blank eyes bright.

'Fifteen years ago Sheriff McAlister ran me out of Monotony. But along with the remnants of Forester's gang I returned and killed him. I didn't pay for that crime, but in my view I paid for my misdemeanours with twelve years of my life. Now I'm a changed man.'

'Twelve years wouldn't go a tenth of the way towards paying for your crimes.' Stirling sneered. 'For a start there's Ben's wife.'

Wendell shrugged. 'Ain't sure which one of my

raiders killed his wife, but I accept the blame for that too.'

'And his boy?'

'Didn't see a child.' Wendell glanced away, his eyes unfocused. 'Although his wife might have been expecting one.'

'How did they die?'

'You know that. You found the bodies.'

'I just want to know if you know.'

Wendell nodded. 'Sheriff McAlister and his wife defended themselves bravely. They killed two of my men before we got into his house. But somebody winged him.' Wendell patted his arm. 'Then we burst in. A bullet to the chest finished him and a bullet to the head finished his wife. Then we let off round after round. When we'd finished, what was left of them would have rattled.'

'Then what did you do?'

'We ate their food and rested up for the night. We buried our two losses in a small copse near the farm, then headed out.'

'Where did you bury Ben and Ruth?'

'We didn't.'

Stirling glanced down. He'd clutched his right hand so hard his fingernails had drawn blood. He closed his eyes and forced his right hand to open.

'I believe you,' he whispered.

'You should. Surprised you even had to ask. But you wanted the truth, so why haven't you asked me the other question?'

Stirling slammed his hands down on his chair arms and moved as if to rise.

'I've heard all I need to hear.'

Wendell raised a hand.

Stirling glared back, then slumped back in the chair.

'You've asked me if I did it. But you ain't asked why I did it.'

Stirling snorted. 'I know the answer to that. You're a sneaky, low-down double-crosser. Ben ran you out of town so you had to kill him.'

'Nope.' Wendell licked his lips, suppressing a grin. 'I killed Sheriff McAlister because *he* was the double-crosser.'

'What?'

'Why do you reckon he didn't run us out of town before? Zachary Forester and me had been here for months.'

Stirling shrugged and this time he stood.

'One man can't face that many.'

'Perhaps not, but he took months before he asked for help. Sheriff Cowie was only fifty miles away and he was a diligent lawman, but he asked for men from out east who'd take weeks to get here.'

Stirling glared down at Wendell. Behind him, Lance edged forward.

'What you saying?'

'I'm saying that Sheriff McAlister was in on our operations. He got a cut of everything we did and in return he gave us leeway.'

'Liar,' Stirling shouted. He turned from Wendell and stormed to the door. With an angry lunge he grabbed the doorknob, then stopped and turned.

'He did,' Wendell said. 'Except he wasn't happy

87

with his cut and wanted more. He played me off against Zachary Forester, offering us both a chance at bigger operations if we double-crossed the other. Zachary turned him down. I didn't and turned on Zachary. When I'd seen him off, McAlister went back on his deal. He threatened to get in lawmen to run me out of town if I didn't agree to his new terms. I called his bluff and he called you in. The rest you know.'

'You forget, Wendell,' Stirling muttered. 'I know when you're lying. And that was a lie.'

'The truth *can* hurt. Fifteen years wanting revenge for the death of a lawman who was even more crooked than the man who killed him.' Wendell laughed, the sound dying with a pained cough. 'What a waste.'

Stirling opened his mouth to shout oaths, then slammed his fist against his thigh. He fought his desire to leap at Wendell and obliterate his smug grin but, with another slam of his fist against his leg, he brushed past Lance, threw open the door and stormed from Wendell's room.

Hoarse chuckling followed him down the corridor.

His mind stayed in a fugue through his hurried journey back to the Palomino Hotel and through his frantic relaying of this tale to Jackson and Wayne.

When he'd finished, Jackson shrugged.

'That tale ain't right and you know it,' he said. 'Ben was the most honest, god-fearing lawman I've known.'

'I know,' Stirling whispered, his heart rate only now slowing. 'I went there to try and goad Wendell into revealing something we could use against him but he just goaded me. It's just a pity I can only kill him the once.'

Stirling threw his hat to the floor and kicked a chair leg. He folded his arms and glared through the window at the road beyond, but in his mind he could only see Wendell's smug grin.

'You won't need to,' Wayne said, breaking the uncomfortable silence. 'Sheriff Yates will arrest Wendell and he'll be swinging by the end of the week.'

'Why?' Stirling muttered. He turned to face Wayne.

Wayne extracted a slip of paper from his jacket pocket.

'Because you and I had the same idea. Except I had more luck. While you were off letting Wendell rile you, I was doing what I used to do fifteen years ago. I investigated the story Wendell told Sheriff Yates. What with the railroad a-coming, we have a telegraph service here.' Wayne grinned and tapped the paper. 'And we have him.'

CHAPTER 11

'Two pair, kings over jacks,' Tom McDonald announced and leaned back in his chair.

Thorpe grunted and let him pounce on the pot.

For the last hour Tom McDonald and Bert Caster had played poker in the Silver Streak Saloon with two of Wendell's gunslingers, Thorpe and Stark. Except Tom and Bert had increasingly monopolized the winning hands.

If the steady losses annoyed the gunslingers, their continual grins gave no hint.

'We got plenty of time to start winning,' Stark said.

'Yeah, the day is yet young,' Thorpe said. He nodded to the table beside theirs. 'But it looks like it's too late for him.'

Tom leaned back to look over his shoulder.

At the table beside them a stinking drunk youngster was sprawled over the table, his cheek pressed into a pool of beer, his glass lying on its side. Two men were dragging him to his feet so they could sit at the table. With grunted complaints they pushed him away.

The youngster tottered a pace, stumbled, then staggered to their table. He swayed, his eyes unfocused, and clattered down to support himself on the table.

'I ain't well,' he murmured, slurring each word. He rubbed his stomach, then heaved.

'Get him out,' Tom whined.

Stark and Thorpe grabbed the youngster and swung him from the table. As the youngster heaved and belched they dragged him to the door, his feet trailing behind him.

Outside, they hurled him down, but the youngster had gripped Stark's shoulder and half-dragged him down too. Stark pried the youngster's fingers from his jacket, then rolled him off the boardwalk and into the road.

The youngster landed in a heap and immediately started snoring.

Stark rocked back his foot ready to kick him, but Thorpe chuckled and shook his head.

'Let him sleep it off. He don't need bruises to go with that sore head he'll have.'

Stark nodded. He glanced down at the youngster, who shifted in his sleep and let out a rasping snore. He patted his hands together and strode back inside to rejoin the poker game.

In the road the youngster lay for a minute.

A bleary eye opened.

He watched the saloon, but nobody emerged or looked through the windows at him. He staggered to his feet. With a shaking hand he grabbed the rail and dragged himself along the road past the saloon.

Nobody within the saloon or out on the road looked at him.

He shrugged his jacket, batted the dust from his clothes, and resumed his walk.

With each pace his gait became more assured and less snaking until by the time he reached the end of the road he was marching at a brisk pace.

At the end of the road a long-coated man stepped out from beside the last building and nodded to him.

'You get it?' he asked.

The youngster smiled, his eyes alive and clear. He lifted his clenched fist and shook it above his head.

'I got it,' he said.

'What is it?' Cassidy asked, looking up from the slip of paper to stare at Wayne. He'd just returned to his office to find the three remaining ex-lawmen waiting for him – and they were smiling.

Wayne grinned, the gleam in his eye that Stirling and Jackson hadn't seen for fifteen years returning.

'The telegram reads, "No". It's short but tells me everything I need to know.'

Cassidy leaned back in his chair and nodded.

'Suppose for me to understand why you're looking so pleased with yourself I need to know what the question was.'

Wayne grinned and with a short grunt levered his stooped body on to the corner of Cassidy's desk. He peered at Cassidy over the top of his half-glasses.

92

'That's right, young lawman. You see I used those instincts that you were so proud about owning. I asked questions. I checked facts. I searched for inconsistencies in Wendell's story.'

Cassidy ran the paper through his hands. 'Stop gloating and just tell me what this means.'

Wayne nodded. 'You told me that Wendell has changed and has paid for his crimes, but that didn't fit in with my previous investigations.'

'What investigations?'

'When Wendell escaped fifteen years ago, we temporarily gave up the chase, but I ensured that if any of my contacts from Kansas to California or from Texas to Montana found him they'd tell me. That's how I knew Wendell Moon was back. An old friend told me he'd passed by. But if Wendell had languished in Leavenworth jail for twelve years, someone had some answers to provide as to why they didn't tell me. So I wired the jail.'

'And the answer was, "No".' Cassidy tapped his chin, then nodded. 'You telling me that the jail ain't heard of him?'

'Yup.'

'Damn,' Cassidy muttered.

'My luck ain't ever changing,' Tom McDonald said, grinning.

Stark grunted and leaned back from the table.

'You won't get a chance to test that. You've fair cleaned me out.'

Thorpe nodded. 'Yeah, me too.'

'But fair is the word,' Tom said.

'Yup. I know.'

Tom reached into his pocket and threw a dollar on the table.

'Then buy yourself a drink to soothe any hard feelings.'

'We got none,' Stark said, taking the coin. 'But we're obliged.'

Tom tipped his hat and with Bert Caster, he sauntered from the saloon. On the boardwalk he took a deep breath, tucked his thumbs in his waistcoat, and sauntered down the road.

Beside him, Bert whistled a contented tune.

Outside the Lone Rider Saloon they debated whether to go inside and play Faro. But they turned and wandered down the road.

Today had been successful and they didn't fancy risking their luck changing.

Tom puffed his chest. The wad of bills in his jacket pocket weighed heavily. He patted the bulge again.

He heard something strange, but he wasn't sure what. He strained his hearing, then realized the strange thing was Bert's silence. He turned to ask why he'd stopped whistling, but Bert had gone.

Tom turned on the spot, looking in all directions. On the deserted road he backtracked, looking left and right into stores and the saloon.

A hand slapped over his mouth and a firm arm over his chest dragged him into an alley. He struggled but a dull thud to his head knocked him to his knees.

He tried to rise but a second blow pummelled him to the ground.

As he flitted in and out of consciousness hands rifled through his pockets and the comforting weight in his pocket slipped away.

CHAPTER 12

'That's an easy one to answer,' Wendell croaked with his arms folded. He glanced at the cells behind Cassidy and grinned. 'Deputy Hearst didn't need to bring me to your office to answer it.'

'He didn't.' Cassidy nodded to Hearst, who backed and sat at his desk. 'But I just wanted the quickest possible answer.'

Wendell rubbed his neck and coughed. He walked in a small circle.

'I ain't sure I need to explain myself. Perhaps I should call Phillip over and we'll check if I have to answer.'

'You can do that. But the last time we talked it was a friendly chat in the saloon. This time it's a formal conversation in my office. I just hope it doesn't have to become an official interrogation with you in one of my cells, which it can be if you want.' Cassidy sauntered to his nearest cell and tapped a firm knuckle against a bar. 'Understand?'

Wendell sneered. 'Didn't expect you to threaten me, Sheriff.'

'I ain't. I protect the innocent, but at the moment I'm wondering whether that includes you.'

'All right. I'll tell you.' Wendell took a deep breath. 'I was in Leavenworth jail, except they didn't call me Wendell Moon.'

'You mean you used an alias?'

Wendell threw back his head and croaked a laugh.

'I mean Wendell Moon *is* an alias.' With the back of his hand, Wendell wiped the smile from his lips. 'I had a colourful youth. When I moved west I adopted an alias to avoid my old troubles.'

'What troubles?'

'Nothing serious. When I left Monotony, I reverted to my real name, Miles Coleman. I spent my time in jail so named.'

'I'll check. And if that doesn't fit the facts—'

'I know.'

'Why have you reverted back to your alias?'

Wendell held his arms wide. 'Miles Coleman served in jail. Wendell Moon didn't. It ain't illegal. You don't need to let it worry you.'

Cassidy rubbed his chin, then nodded. 'All right. You can go.'

Wendell returned his usual grin, then sauntered from his office, rubbing his neck.

Cassidy watched him leave, then turned to Hearst.

'That sound plausible to you?' he asked.

Hearst shrugged. 'I don't know, but he didn't lie when you first asked him about his past. In fact he volunteered the information about serving a jail sentence when he was well within his rights to keep quiet.'

'He lied about serving his sentence under a different name.'

'Nope. You didn't ask him about that.'

'You're right.' Cassidy sighed. 'He ain't lied, but he ain't volunteering the whole truth. I reckon—'

The door creaked open and Tom McDonald wandered in holding his head with one hand and propping up Bert Caster with the other.

Cassidy and Hearst dashed from behind their desks and helped them to chairs. Cassidy whistled under his breath.

'You two have seen some trouble.'

'Yeah,' Tom said. 'And the day started so well. We won fifty dollars apiece from Wendell Moon's gunslingers.'

Cassidy removed Tom's hand and dabbed at the reddening bump on his head. He glanced at his hand, seeing only a smear of blood.

'Don't reckon it's anything serious.'

'What hurts most is we didn't get a chance to fight back.'

Bert prodded the back of his head. He winced, then snorted.

'What hurts most,' he said, 'is we didn't get to spend our winnings.'

Cassidy nodded. 'You any idea who did it?'

Tom and Bert glanced at each other, sharing a nod.

'Wendell's gunslingers ambushed us,' Tom said.

'You see them do it?' Cassidy asked.

'Nope, but they followed us when we left the Silver Streak Saloon, ambushed us, and stole back their money.'

'The way things are going today I ain't got time for surmising.' Cassidy raised his voice. 'Did you see them attack you?'

'They attacked us from behind but it was them.'

Cassidy winced. 'Ain't got room for buts. Just because you beat them at poker, don't mean they stole their money back. Plenty of people would have seen you win.'

Hearst nodded. 'Yeah, and that's what they'll say if we go to them.'

'But I have proof.' Tom extracted a silver moon badge from his pocket and placed it on Cassidy's desk. 'I searched around when I came to and found this beside Bert. It must have fallen off when they attacked us.'

Cassidy looked at Hearst.

'Stirling's people playing tricks again?' he asked.

Hearst shook his head. 'Nope. They were waiting in here for the last hour or more.'

'Then Stirling was right,' he muttered, poking the badge around his desk. 'Trouble escalates when Wendell Moon is around.'

Wayne Stone stood outside Ben McAlister's old house, staring at the derelict building. In his right hand he held a shovel, but his gaze was not for this time.

He shook himself, freeing the bad thoughts and returning him to the present to see the building the way it appeared today, and not as he remembered it in the days when a family lived there.

With the supporting timbers stolen for other houses the roof had caved in, but enough of the adobe walls remained for someone who could cope with the old ghosts to try to live there again.

Despite the passage of years the disgust he felt burned his throat and Wayne turned away. He forced himself to concentrate on his reason for this journey.

Wayne hadn't put all his faith in his one discovery. Experience suggested that Wendell would talk his way out of the inconsistency in his jail story and he needed to find another flaw to maintain the pressure on his lies.

The information Stirling had learned while Wendell goaded him was as good a place to start as any, so he'd left Stirling and Jackson in the Palomino Hotel and ridden here on his own.

He paced around the outside of the house to stand on the south side.

As Wendell had said, a copse nestled in a hollow two hundred yards from the house. With deliberate pacing, Wayne sauntered to the copse.

At the copse he glanced around, searching for a likely spot for an impromptu grave. This expedition was probably hopeless – even if he found the remains of Wendell Moon's gang that died here, he probably wouldn't find anything to link them to Wendell.

But he was sure of one thing, something that remained from his judging days.

When someone told you a story, you checked it out and you carried on checking out everything that you subsequently unearthed. If the original story contained a lie, before too long discrepancies mounted and you reached the truth.

Wayne selected a mound of rough earth mixed with a mass of rotted leaves and slammed the shovel into it.

For ten minutes he worked before he admitted that the mound was just an old anthill. He sauntered to the next tree and dug into another mound. He let the recent irritations erode as he lost himself in manual work.

Warmth prickled on the back of his neck – he felt as if someone were looking at him.

He straightened, his back giving a sharp twinge, and swung the shovel on to his shoulder. He turned.

Stark and Thorpe sat astride their horses, grinning down at him.

'Howdy,' Stark said.

Wayne gulped back his surprise. He pushed his glasses up his nose and forced a smile.

'What you doing out here?' he asked with his calmest voice.

'We could ask you the same question.'

'I'm digging.' Wayne rolled the shovel from his shoulder and held it before him. 'What're you doing?'

'Watching you dig.' Stark leapt from his horse. 'But you ain't much good at it. Perhaps I ought to save an old-timer's tired arms and help.'

Wayne fingered a knot in his biceps, receiving a sharp twinge. He shrugged and held out the shovel.

'Be my guest.'

Stark took the shovel and rolled his shoulders. He looked at the hole Wayne had created and squared up to it.

Wayne backed up a pace.

Stark took a deep breath, then swung the shovel sideways, hitting Wayne across the jaw with the flat of the blade. The shovel rang with a dull clang as Wayne collapsed on his back.

Stark stood over Wayne. He sneered and brought the shovel down on Wayne's forehead, this time hitting with the point of the blade. He pried the shovel away and slammed it down again and again.

'That's enough,' Thorpe shouted.

Stark swung the shovel down one more time, then stood back. He grinned up at Thorpe and held out the bloodstained shovel.

'I reckon I've done enough shovelling for now.' He gestured to the hole. 'Old-timer's started a hole. You can finish it.'

CHAPTER 13

From the boardwalk opposite the Silver Streak Saloon, Zachary and Henry watched the two deputies escort Stark and Thorpe across the road.

Ten minutes earlier the gunslingers had galloped back into Monotony and disappeared into the Coronet Hotel. Within minutes, the deputies had dragged them outside.

Stark and Thorpe scowled at each other but walked with their hands high. Each deputy carried a gunbelt in his outstretched hands.

With the deputies at the back, the group filed into the sheriff's office.

The door slammed shut, the sound echoed with a sigh from Zachary. He turned to Henry.

'I can see,' he said, smiling, 'that I'll like working for you.'

Henry nodded. A wide grin broke out.

'Yeah,' he said. 'And now there's just the one.'

'We've done nothing wrong,' Stark muttered from his cell.

Cassidy stared at him through the bars and shook his head.

'For a man with your job, that ain't likely.'

Stark kicked at the cell bars. 'It's the truth.'

'I'm still checking out your story, but from what I've heard so far, nobody can confirm where you were when Tom and Bert were attacked.'

'We weren't in the saloon. But we weren't with those men.'

'Then where were you?'

Stark glanced at Thorpe and hung his head. 'On business.'

'So Wendell's your only alibi?'

'Not all our business involves Mr Moon.'

Cassidy tipped back his hat and backed from the cells, shaking his head.

'You ain't making this easy. You have no alibi and you ain't offering any explanations. That just leaves me to investigate. So if I find evidence that you're innocent, I'll let you go.' Cassidy sat behind his desk. With an exaggerated gesture he locked his hands behind his neck. 'I'll be investigating as fast as I can.'

'We protect Mr Moon from men like Stirling and Jackson.' Stark rattled the bars, finding no give. 'But if you won't let us do that, you'll have to do our job for us.'

'I always protect the innocent.' Cassidy grinned and clumped his feet on the desk. He rocked on his back chair legs. 'And I'll be doing it right here until I get some answers from you.'

Stark grunted and paced to the back wall to throw himself on to the bunk.

For five minutes Cassidy rocked his chair back and forth, then Phillip Tannin, Wendell's attorney, bustled into the office. Cassidy stopped rocking and winced.

'This is most unfortunate, most unfortunate indeed,' Phillip said, 'but I'm here to represent my two associates.'

'No need. I ain't charged them yet.' Cassidy stretched and stifled a false yawn. 'I'm just holding them while I investigate further.'

Phillip pointed at the cells. 'But unless my eyes deceive me, they are in your cells.'

'And I'll let them out if I can prove they're innocent.' Cassidy clattered his chair down and stood. He paced round his desk to stare down at the plump attorney. 'And the longer I talk to you, the longer it'll take.'

Phillip stepped back a pace and passed his small briefcase from hand to hand.

'I don't believe they should be incarcerated while you conduct inquiries.'

Cassidy snorted and stared down at the bald spot on the top of Phillip's head.

'Ain't you got forms to fill in or something?'

'I have too much to do.' Phillip counted off his woes on his podgy fingers. 'I have these men to worry about, land documents to sort, and Mr Whittler's next of kin to track down to see who inherits. It's too much – most unfortunate.'

Cassidy narrowed his eyes. 'Mr Whittler's next of kin?'

'Ah.' Phillip gulped. 'You do know about that

unfortunate problem, don't you?'

'What problem?'

Phillip turned his briefcase over twice, then extracted a handkerchief to mop his brow.

'Mr Whittler's family were killed recently – probably by marauders.'

'When?' Cassidy snapped.

'I don't know. Mr Moon said that when he arrived at Mr Whittler's farm to discuss the land purchase they were dead – murdered most horribly.'

'That sounds . . .' Cassidy rubbed the bridge of his nose, then sighed and pulled his hat low. 'This looks bad for Mr Moon.'

'I deplore the inference. Mr Moon will honour his agreement in full to Mr Whittler's beneficiaries. Mr Moon won't benefit from this.' Phillip sighed. 'It just adds more complications to a simple deal – most unfortunate.'

Cassidy slammed his hands on his hips. 'Then why did he say nothing?'

Phillip backed and mopped his damp cheeks. 'I guess that he assumed you knew so—'

'Be quiet. I've suffered his half-truths and I ain't listening to yours.' Cassidy aimed a firm finger at the door. 'Now get out!'

Phillip flushed. He gulped and hung his head, then bustled from Cassidy's office.

Cassidy paced in a circle, letting just enough of his anger subside, then stormed from his office and across the road. As he reached the middle of the road, from the Palomino Hotel, Stirling angled in to him.

'Get out of my way!' Cassidy roared, and thrust his head down further.

Stirling edged to the side and stood in his way. Cassidy slid to a halt.

'I've just heard you've arrested two of Wendell's gunslingers. Glad to see you're seeing sense – finally.'

Cassidy moved to push past Stirling, then stopped and glared at him.

'I ain't seeing that much sense because you ain't in my cells either. If you don't stop obstructing me, that'll change.'

Stirling glared back, then stood to the side.

Cassidy brushed by Stirling and towards the Coronet Hotel.

'I know you don't want my advice but Wendell is in the Silver Streak Saloon,' Stirling shouted after Cassidy but the sheriff set his shoulders high and strode into the hotel.

Stirling turned, but from the corner of his eye he saw a long-coated man pull his hat low and sidle into the Silver Streak Saloon, glancing at Stirling as he pushed through the doors.

Stirling shook himself and turned. He strode back to the Palomino Hotel. Jackson emerged to stand on the boardwalk.

'Reckon as time's running out for Wendell,' Jackson said.

Stirling nodded. 'Sheriff's about to have another word with him, and he's mighty annoyed.'

'You reckon that Wendell's excuse for him not being in Leavenworth jail just turned up blank?'

'That or any one of the other lies. And we still have

107

to hear what Wayne uncovers from Ben's old house.'

Jackson rubbed his hands and smiled.

From the Coronet Hotel Cassidy emerged, his shoulders hunched forward and his gait quick.

Jackson chuckled and leaned on the rail.

'Reckon as Cassidy wants Wendell nearly as bad as we do now.'

Stirling matched Jackson's chuckle, then slammed a hand on his forehead.

'Zachary Forester,' he whispered.

Jackson snorted. 'If that old scoundrel is still alive, he probably wants Wendell more than we do.'

'No,' Stirling muttered. 'I just recognized a man who went into the saloon. It was Zachary Forester.'

CHAPTER 14

From across the road, Stirling and Jackson stormed to the Silver Streak Saloon.

Ten yards from the saloon Cassidy slid to a halt and lifted a hand.

'I told you two to stay away from Wendell,' he shouted.

Jackson rocked back and forth on his heels. He shrugged.

'We'll stay away, if that's what you want.'

Cassidy nodded, then narrowed his eyes.

'Then why were you heading for the saloon?'

'No reason.'

Cassidy considered Jackson, then turned to the saloon.

'This is your last warning,' he shouted over his shoulder, 'stay away from Wendell. I'm dealing with him.'

Stirling and Jackson grunted their acceptance, but when Cassidy took a pace, Jackson coughed.

'Don't go in the saloon,' he murmured.

Cassidy turned back. 'Why?'

'Just stay outside for another minute and our problems will be over.'

'You'd better explain that one to me.'

Jackson folded his arms and turned away, so Cassidy turned to Stirling.

'Zachary Forester just headed into the saloon,' Stirling said. 'I thought that rat died years ago but as he didn't, Wendell's future ain't looking promising.'

Cassidy winced. Without further comment, he stormed down the road but, hearing Jackson and Stirling following, he turned back.

'You two stay away or you'll be behind bars.'

'You'll need help if you're planning on separating Zachary Forester and Wendell Moon.'

'I don't need the kind of help you'll provide.' Cassidy turned to the saloon and lowered his voice to a menacing growl. 'If you step one foot inside that saloon, it'll be your last.'

'You can't threaten two lawmen,' Stirling shouted at Cassidy's receding back.

'You're ex-lawmen,' Cassidy shouted as he reached the boardwalk.

A gunshot blasted in the saloon, two more following. Someone screamed and the saloon window exploded outwards as a man leapt through it.

Cassidy jumped to the side of the swing-doors. He knelt and peered under the doors.

Inside, the customers had backed to the walls.

Cassidy pulled his gun and nudged through the doors to stand beside the doorway. The doors swung closed behind him.

By the wall Wendell and Lance were crouched

behind two upturned tables. Lance peered around the side to face the bar.

Cassidy looked to the bar. A hat of someone hiding behind the bar just protruded halfway along it.

'Zachary Forester,' Cassidy muttered, 'this is Sheriff Cassidy Yates. Come on out.'

Zachary snorted. 'I ain't listening to a lawman – not when I have Wendell in my sights.'

Cassidy glanced to the wall where Wendell cowered behind a table.

'That man attacked Mr Moon,' Lance muttered. 'I was just defending him.'

While keeping the bar in view, Cassidy edged sideways across the saloon to them, throwing out each leg with care, then shuffling the other up to meet it. When he reached the upturned table, he glanced down at the cowering Wendell over the top of table.

'I'll ensure you come to no harm. Come out. If Zachary does anything, he'll die.'

'I know,' Lance muttered. 'I'm protecting Mr Moon.'

'You ain't, because you're putting down your gun.' Cassidy faced the bar. He aimed his gun at the protruding hat and raised his voice. 'Then Zachary is putting his gun on the bar and coming out too.'

'That ain't happening,' Lance said.

'Like the man said,' Zachary shouted, 'that ain't happening.'

'It is.' Cassidy swung his gun in a steady arc to aim it at Lance. 'Because I say so.'

Lance stared down the barrel of the gun. He sneered.

'You wouldn't shoot an innocent man,' he said.

'I wouldn't, but I'll shoot an armed man who plans to kill another.'

'Even an outlaw like Zachary Forester?'

From the corner of his eye, Cassidy glanced at Wendell.

'Yeah. I'd defend even the worst outlaw in certain circumstances.'

Lance glared back, but Wendell whispered an order from the corner of his mouth. Lance released his grip on his gun. The gun swung on a finger, then clattered to the floor.

Cassidy kicked the gun away a few feet and aimed his gun to the bar.

'Zachary, you have a gun on two unarmed men. That ain't a healthy position for you.'

A long sigh emerged from behind the bar. Zachary raised his hands, his gun pointing to the ceiling. Moving slowly he stood. He glared across the saloon at Wendell, then glanced at Cassidy's gun.

With a slow shake of his head, he placed his gun on the bar, then raised his hand.

'That good enough?'

'Yup. Now come out from behind the bar and walk outside with your hands on your head. You'll get your gun back when you're on your horse and ready to head out of town.'

With slow paces Zachary strode from behind the bar. He glanced at the door, then strode two paces closer to Cassidy.

'This ain't over, Sheriff.'

'I guessed as such, but—'

Something moved beside Cassidy. He turned.

Lance was edging his hand down to the gun on the floor, but seeing Cassidy turn, he leapt on it, his move like lightning.

Cassidy kicked out, the toe of his boot catching the gun as Lance's grasping fingers closed on it. He stamped down, just missing Lance's fingers and, as Lance flinched back, he slugged him backhanded with his gun hand for him to fly back against the wall.

With a dull thud Lance's head crunched into the wall and rocked down slack-mouthed on to his chest.

Rapid footsteps sounded behind him. Cassidy spun round.

With his head down Zachary was charging across the saloon. Cassidy swung his gun towards him but Zachary bundled into Cassidy, knocking the gun to the floor. Cassidy grabbed Zachary's shoulders and tried to pull him down, but Zachary squirmed from his grip and took a long pace towards Wendell, his hands held like great claws.

With a desperate lunge, Cassidy grabbed Zachary's midriff.

To try to free himself Zachary crunched his elbow back into Cassidy's cheek. Cassidy's head snapped back, his hat falling to the floor. Cassidy fell, but he grabbed Zachary's arm and yanked him down to his knees. Cassidy rolled to his knees. He grabbed Zachary's shoulder, spun him around, and slugged him full on the jaw.

Zachary shrugged off the blow and head butted Cassidy.

Cassidy saw the blow coming and jerked back his

head, but Zachary's forehead still slammed into his chin.

While Cassidy rolled back dazed, he heard someone shout indistinctly. With his vision dark he staggered to his feet and threw a punch at Zachary, the blow whistling through air. He righted himself and shook his head, clearing his vision.

With his hands raised Zachary stood before him.

Cassidy looked to Wendell, to the unconscious Lance, then to the door – in the doorway, Stirling stood with his gun pointed at Zachary's back. Jackson was at his side, his gun on Wendell.

'I told you to stay outside,' Cassidy muttered.

Stirling grinned. 'And we'll go when our fellow lawman doesn't need our help any more.'

'Then I'm obliged,' Cassidy said.

'And I'm much obliged to you too,' Wendell shouted from behind his table. 'Zachary would have finished me if you hadn't have stopped him.'

Stirling nodded. 'I was just saving you for me.'

'Quit the posturing,' Cassidy shouted. He retrieved his hat and gun from the floor, then pointed to the door.

With a last glare at Wendell, Zachary strode across the saloon and through the door.

Cassidy grabbed Zachary's gun from the bar, then followed him. Outside, Cassidy nodded to Stirling and Jackson.

'My warning still holds. Stay away from Wendell.'

Jackson sneered but Stirling nodded.

'We understand,' Stirling said.

Cassidy turned to Zachary. He punched out five

bullets, then held out Zachary's gun.

'You too. That was your only warning. Stay out of town.'

Zachary glared back at the Cassidy. 'You've just made the biggest mistake of your life, Sheriff.'

'And you didn't listen to my warning.' Cassidy beckoned Deputy Hearst, who was trotting across the road to the saloon.

Hearst slid to a halt. 'Yeah, boss?'

'Throw this one in the cells.'

Zachary snorted as Hearst grabbed his arm.

'Sheriff,' he muttered. 'You just made another big mistake.'

Cassidy shrugged and turned to Jackson.

'Zachary Forester ain't that tough,' Jackson said. 'Even Wendell saw him off before, so—'

'Stop!' Cassidy roared. 'I have had enough of you and your petty squabbling.'

'This ain't petty. Wendell killed a lawman – in case you forgot.'

'I ain't interested in feuds from fifteen years ago. I only care about what's happening now.'

'If you dismiss the death of a lawman, you ain't any kind of lawman.' Jackson sneered. 'Or man.'

With his heart thudding Cassidy tipped back his hat and glared at the two ex-lawmen, then turned to watch Hearst drag Zachary into the sheriff's office. When the door slammed shut, his heartbeat had slowed a mite and he turned back.

'I ain't standing for that sort of talk from you any more. I'm more of a lawman than you'll ever be. You wanted to let Zachary and Wendell fight it out.'

Cassidy took a deep breath. 'No innocent people died in the saloon, but that was only through luck. Soon, that luck will run out.'

'Wendell ain't innocent,' Stirling muttered.

'I didn't mean him!' Cassidy roared, thrusting his face to within scant inches of Stirling's face. 'I mean the townsfolk of Monotony, who ain't interested in your feud. It's clearly been a long time since you were a lawman because you've forgotten them.'

Stirling winced and forced a begrudging nod.

'You're right. What do you want us to do?'

Cassidy took long breaths, calming his anger.

'While I decide what to do with you, head for your hotel, stay there, and give me no reason to think you ain't law-abiding men.'

'And what are you doing?'

'It ain't your place to ask, ex-lawman.' With that Cassidy turned and stormed into the Silver Streak Saloon, leaving Stirling and Jackson to share irritated glances.

Wendell smiled when he saw Cassidy.

'Let me thank you, Sheriff,' he croaked, batting dust from his knees.

'Don't bother,' Cassidy muttered. 'Stirling was right about you. Where you are, trouble ain't far away.'

Wendell shook his head. He righted the fallen tables and chairs. With his usual smile now returning, he gestured to one of the chairs and sat in the other.

'None of that trouble was anything to do with me.'

Cassidy glanced at the chair and folded his arms.

116

'I can't prove it was your fault, but I have plenty of questions.'

'Ask and I will answer – once I've fetched Phillip from the hotel.'

Cassidy grunted. 'I'm sure you will. But I ain't had a gunfight in a month and no deaths since I became sheriff. Then you arrive. Now I have five bodies and two ambushes and a whole lot more besides.'

'None of which has anything to do with me. If you look at this from my viewpoint, your problems started when Stirling and the others arrived.'

'You're right and for that reason I'm testing a theory.' Cassidy wandered to the prone Lance. With a steady rhythm he kicked him in the side until he twitched and shuffled back from the blows. Cassidy turned back to Wendell. 'Your employee is now conscious. You have business in Redemption City and I'd be obliged if you'd deal with it. If the trouble continues when you've left, I'll accept you had nothing to do with it and you're welcome to stop here on your way back west.'

Wendell raised his eyebrows. 'Are you running me out of town?'

'Nope. I'm *asking* you to leave town.' Cassidy lowered his hat and narrowed his eyes. 'But I'm only asking once.'

'But I still have business to conclude here.'

'As you've complained, I'll stop asking.' Cassidy took a deep breath. 'Pay your hotel bill, get on your horse, and head on out of here. If I find proof you've anything to do with the trouble here, I'll come fetch you.'

117

'You can't do that,' Wendell croaked, rubbing his sore neck.

Cassidy smiled. He tipped back his hat and placed his hands on his hips.

'I just did.'

Lance jumped to his feet and took a long pace towards Cassidy but Wendell shook his head.

'There's no need for trouble. I'll leave.'

'I know you will.'

With a few mutterings, Wendell and Lance strode from the saloon, Cassidy following.

'Ain't no need to follow,' Wendell said on the boardwalk. 'I said I'll go.'

'Trouble is, I ain't trusting your word any more.'

Wendell shook his head and strode down the boardwalk to the Coronet Hotel. Cassidy followed three paces behind. Inside Lance dashed up to Wendell's room and collected their belongings while Wendell slammed a wad of bills on the reception desk.

'Sheriff,' he said when he'd checked out, 'I'll be obliged if you'd fetch Stark and Thorpe.'

'They're staying. They still have questions to answer.'

'Then Phillip will have to stay to help answer them.'

Cassidy shrugged. 'I have no problem with him. I do have a problem with you.'

Wendell glared back at Cassidy, then scurried outside to his horse. When Lance joined him, they glanced around, then rode out of town without looking back, heading east.

Cassidy watched them leave, then strode to the Palomino Hotel. In the dining room at the back, Stirling and Jackson sat around a pot of coffee.

Stirling looked up. 'Sheriff, reckon as you deserve an apology. You were right. We forgot a lawman's prime duty and put innocent people at risk with our actions. We're sorry.'

Cassidy nodded. 'Then I'm glad we can part on good terms.'

Jackson jumped to his feet, knocking over his coffee mug.

'What do you mean by that?' he shouted.

'I've decided that I've had enough of the trouble around here. I ain't sure what your involvement in it is, but as ex-lawmen I trust you to come quietly if I find out that you were to blame.' Cassidy pointed outside. 'So pay your hotel bills, get on your horses, and head on out of here.'

Jackson rolled forward. 'You're running us out of town. You two-bit—'

'Any more complaints and you'll join Wendell's men in my cells.'

Jackson spat on the floor. 'You're defending a lawman's killer and—'

Stirling patted Jackson's shoulder. 'This is Cassidy's town and we've pushed him enough. Let's go. There'll be other days.'

Jackson shrugged. 'We have to wait for Wayne to return.'

Cassidy shook his head. 'I'm treating you all the same. Soon as he returns, I'll tell him where you headed and he'll be leaving town too.'

119

With muttered oaths Jackson stormed to his room. Stirling glanced at Cassidy then followed him.

Cassidy wandered outside and leaned back against a post.

Stirling was the first to emerge. He contemplated Cassidy, then forced a wan smile.

'I'll apologize for what Jackson said. He doesn't mean to argue. We know you're trying to keep the peace in a difficult situation. It's a pity that sometimes a lawman's duties force him to protect the wrong man.'

'I'll accept your apology. I don't know who is right and who is wrong. I just treat everyone the same.'

Jackson joined them on the boardwalk and snorted.

'You treat ex-lawmen like outlaws,' he said, 'and lawmen killers like victims. That ain't any kind of justice.'

Cassidy sighed. 'I've had plenty of trouble here and I can't work out who is responsible, so like I say, I'm treating everyone the same.'

Jackson sneered and strode to his horse, but Stirling stayed, contemplating Cassidy's bunch-jawed expression.

'You treat everyone the same, you say?' he asked.

Cassidy rocked his right leg up and batted dirt from his boot.

'Yup.'

Stirling rubbed his chin. 'There's trouble and you don't know who caused it. We say it's Wendell and Wendell says it's us, but you run us out of town.'

Cassidy pushed from the post and tipped back his hat.

'Yup.'

'But if you treat everyone the same—'

'You're approaching my time-limit. You have another minute's grace, then I'll escort you out of town at the end of a gun.' Cassidy widened his eyes as he glared at Stirling. 'Wendell didn't need two warnings.'

Stirling chuckled. He tipped his hat and mounted his horse.

'I reckon Monotony is in good hands. Ben McAlister would be proud of you. We'll be heading east . . .' Stirling lifted his reins, then lowered them, '. . . if that's all right with you.'

'Ain't caring where you go. I just don't want to show you ex-lawmen the discourtesy of escorting you out of town.' Cassidy pointed with a firm finger down the road. 'Now go!'

Stirling stared at Cassidy's inscrutable expression. He glanced at the pointing finger and followed its direction to look down the road.

The finger pointed east.

Stirling nodded. 'East it is.'

CHAPTER 15

Sheriff Cassidy Yates watched Stirling gallop down the road to catch up with Jackson.

Deputy Hearst joined Cassidy.

'You just treated them all the same,' he said.

'Yup,' Cassidy said. 'I've also reconsidered Zachary Forester's punishment. Tell him I'm letting him go, but he ain't welcome here either.'

Hearst contemplated Cassidy. 'Should he go in any particular direction?'

'I don't care as long he stays away.'

Hearst nodded. 'But east would be a good way to go?'

'It's as good as any. Then head out to James Whittler's farm. I reckon you'll find some bad news there.' Cassidy turned, then turned back. 'Before you go, tell Giles to watch out for Stark and Thorpe. They'll be desperate to get out now.'

'You ain't planning on being around either?'

'Nope. I'll be scouting around. I have a feeling that something is about to happen out east.'

'And you'll just make sure it turns out right?'

Cassidy glanced at Hearst and headed for his horse.

'I don't know what you mean.'

'Hey, Deputy,' Stark shouted. 'How much longer do we have to stink away in here?'

Deputy Giles snorted. 'Until we get to the truth.'

'Then let us out. We did nothing.'

'And when we know that for sure, we'll let you go.'

'Where's the sheriff?'

'He's investigating, as is Hearst.' Giles sauntered from the cells and sat behind Cassidy's desk. 'Or perhaps they ain't. Either way, I'd get comfortable. You ain't going anywhere soon.'

As Stark muttered oaths, the door swung open and Phillip Tannin bustled in.

'Oh dear, oh dear, oh dear,' he whined. 'I hear we've had some bother and Mr Moon has had to curtail his business here.'

'Yup,' Giles said.

Phillip mopped his brow. 'This is most unfortunate, most unfortunate.'

'Not for us.' Giles folded his arms and leaned back in his chair, grinning. 'We don't have to cope with your conniving boss any longer.'

'You have misunderstood Mr Moon but this is most inconvenient. I've documents to draft and Mr Whittler's death doesn't make things any easier, I can tell you.'

'I'll be sure to pass on your condolences.'

Phillip pouted. 'I didn't mean that, but this is most unfortunate.'

'You already said.' Giles sighed. 'Cassidy says you're free to come and go as you please, but if you want to follow your boss, he went east.'

'I know where he went. We have appointments in Redemption City, but getting there is the problem.'

'You could hurry after him, or make your own way later. You could use the coach. We get one a week.' Giles smiled. 'Next one is in four days.'

Phillip sauntered round to the side of the desk and pointed at the cells.

'And will those gentlemen still be detained then?'

Giles stayed leaned back in his chair until Phillip looked at him.

'Can't say. Cassidy is still investigating.'

Phillip hung his head. 'Most unfortunate. Most unfortunate indeed.'

Phillip bustled to the door, then stopped with his hand on the door. He rocked back and forth, then sidled back to the desk.

'You're a lawman, right?'

Giles chuckled. 'You're an observant man for an attorney.'

Phillip's cheeks reddened. 'Well, I ain't had much need for weapons and such like, but with this most unfortunate situation, I'd welcome some advice.'

Giles tipped back his hat. 'Which is?'

'If Mr Moon's men won't be available I'll have to make my own way to Redemption City and you hear about vagabonds and ruffians waylaying travellers on the trail. I will need to be in a position to defend myself. What kind of weapon would you suggest I get?'

'Vagabonds and ruffians,' Giles murmured. He whistled under his breath. 'Yeah, you do get them on the trail, but I don't reckon you'll stand a chance if they waylay you. Just hand over your valuables and think yourself lucky if they don't kill you.'

'That would still be most unfortunate.' Phillip nodded at the deputy's holster. 'I'd prefer another option. I know that's a Peacemaker. Would you suggest I get one of those?'

'It's an awful big weapon for you.' Giles chuckled and patted his holster. 'Rosie Jenkins in the Lone Rider Saloon keeps a dinky pistol in her garter. That type of weapon might suit you more.'

Phillip mopped his sweating brow. 'I fear that was a jest at my expense. But perhaps you have the right idea. A small concealed weapon might be better protection for me.'

Giles yawned. 'Perhaps it might.'

'I'm glad you think so.'

Phillip straightened his cuffs, then gave the barest of nudges.

Giles glimpsed steel, but by then the small pistol was in Phillip's hand and blasting lead twice in quick succession.

Giles doubled over, clutching his chest, and fell from his chair.

Phillip stood over the body, confirming that Giles was still. He shrugged again. The elastic in his sleeve pulled the small pistol back.

'Yeah,' Phillip muttered, a gruffness replacing his former tentative voice. 'Most unfortunate.'

'Quit gloating and get over here,' Stark yelled from the cells.

Phillip grabbed the cell keys and dashed to the cells. With a few deft movements he unlocked the doors.

Within seconds both men were free. They both patted Phillip's back, then rifled through the office, collecting their guns.

'You coming?' Stark asked.

'I'll follow on behind,' Phillip grunted.

With a last nod to Phillip, Stark and Thorpe stormed from the office. They charged to the Coronet Hotel, mounted their horses, and galloped from town, heading east.

Phillip strode out on to the boardwalk and watched them leave. With a shrug he mounted his horse and swung it round to head north.

'East might be most unfortunate,' he whispered.

CHAPTER 16

'Where you going?' Jackson asked. 'Redemption City is this way.'

Stirling pulled his horse to a halt. He looked up the grass-coated northern trail into the prairies – Ben's old house was three miles away – then turned to Jackson.

'You know why.'

Jackson shrugged. 'No reason for Wendell to go there. He'll be heading to Redemption City.'

'Two of Wendell's gunslingers are in Cassidy's cells and I don't reckon Wendell's concluded his business in Monotony. He has to stay close, and Redemption City is too far.'

'Even so, he'd find somewhere else to hide out.'

Stirling snorted. 'You know Wendell. It ain't enough for him to beat you. He has to rub your nose in it. Why else would he come back to Monotony, except to prove something? Hiding out at the house where he killed a lawman and his family is just the sort of thing he'd do.'

Jackson nodded and without further comment

they headed from the main trail.

Three miles out, they approached the ramshackle house. It nestled on the edge of a meadow, which if Ben's plan had come to fruition would now be farmed land.

'It looks deserted,' Jackson said. 'Perhaps you were wrong. About the only thing that's bigger than Wendell's cockiness is his cowardice.'

'You might be right, but. . . .' From close to, a horse neighed. 'You hear that?'

'My hearing ain't gone yet. They're here.'

They approached the house. Stirling nodded to the side.

'Head for that copse, but edge from the trail slowly as if we were heading there all along.'

Jackson shook his head. 'Got no reason to go there. Wendell will know we're heading to the house.'

'Perhaps, but we got no cover and besides, that copse is where Wendell said he buried his dead gang members, so we could be heading there to search for them.'

Jackson pulled his horse to the side. They headed to the copse, but from the corners of their eyes they still searched for any movements within the house. Despite hearing the occasional whinny, which appeared to be coming from behind the house, they didn't see Wendell and Lance.

At the copse, they dismounted.

They were two hundred yards from the house, side-on, but the house lacked a roof so anyone peering over the crumbled walls would see them.

'What now?' Jackson asked.

Stirling scratched his head, then winced. Beside a tree there was a hole and beside that there was a fresh soil pile.

Stirling stared at the pile, then hung his head.

'Oh no,' he muttered and dashed to the pile. He scraped away handfuls of soil, then flinched and fell back to let Jackson see what he'd unearthed.

Jackson glanced down at the protruding arm.

'Wayne?'

Stirling batted soil off the body's hand to reveal liver spots.

'Yeah. It just has to be.' Stirling rolled back on his haunches, shaking his head. 'Told the old fool he'd get himself killed by coming along.'

'No time for that.' Jackson patted his holster. 'We have to sort this.'

Stirling nodded and pushed to his feet.

'We need a—'

Gunshots echoed from the house. They both turned, pulling their guns as they dropped to their knees.

From the trail they'd just travelled down, two riders hurtled towards the house. With his poor eyesight and from so far away, Stirling couldn't tell who they were, but one man was thin and young. The elder man's long coat fluttered behind him.

'Zachary Forester,' Jackson muttered.

'This is a good distraction.'

With a last nod to each other, they dashed for the house as fast as their aged legs would carry them.

The riders slid to halt, lay down a peppering of

gunfire, then headed for the derelict barn. They swung their horses around the back of the barn, dismounted and vaulted the low walls to hide inside.

With the distraction over Stirling and Jackson threw themselves beside the only cover – a tangle of bushes.

'We ain't got much hope from here,' Jackson muttered, peering out at the house.

'But we outnumber them now – four to two.'

'Zachary is only on our side indirectly. We can't trust him to help us. We might as well be on our own.' Jackson sighed. 'So I'll talk to him. I'll get him to fight on our side.'

'We ain't siding with that—'

'Don't say it,' Jackson muttered, lifting a hand. 'I have had enough of this. I don't care how we do this as long as someone gets Wendell.'

For long moments Stirling glared back, then nodded.

'Agreed.'

Jackson shuffled from the bush. With his head down he headed from the house. In a long arc he dashed to the back of the barn. When the barn blocked his view of the house, he hunkered down beside a rock heap, thirty yards back, and wheezed until he caught his breath.

'Zachary,' he shouted. 'I ain't here for you. Let me in and we can work together.'

Long moments passed. Zachary edged his head over the side of the nearest wall.

'We ain't together.'

Jackson shook his head. 'I'm against Wendell, and

that makes us together.'

Zachary snorted. 'So put down that gun and I'll—'

In the barn a youngster appeared and patted Zachary's shoulder. Zachary turned to talk to him. Low muttering sounded.

By his rock heap Jackson scratched his head.

His innards turned to ice.

He rolled to his feet and staggered a pace.

'Henry,' he said. 'What in tarnation are you doing here?'

Henry glanced over the wall, then dropped. Zachary swung his gun on to the wall.

'Stay right there, lawman,' he shouted.

Jackson snorted. He holstered his gun and paced to the barn with his hands raised to his chest. At the wall, he swung over it, brushed past Zachary, and faced up to the youngster, who hid against the opposite wall.

'I asked what Stirling's boy is doing here.'

Henry gulped. 'Same as you – getting Wendell.'

'You've been helping this man?' Jackson gestured to Zachary, who still had his gun trained on him. 'Do you know who he is?'

Henry rolled to his haunches and nodded. 'I do and after today we'll part company. But for now I'm helping to save pa's life – and yours.'

'You'll do nothing but get yourself killed.'

Henry wandered a pace closer to Jackson. 'I have a better chance than Frank Taylor had. And I have a better chance than either you or pa.'

Zachary chuckled and stalked round to face Jackson.

131

'This kid talks a whole lot of sense.'

Jackson rubbed his eyes, shaking his head.

'What a ridiculous team! No wonder Wendell has survived for so long when he faces this sort of opposition.'

'Perhaps, but the kid's done all right. If he wants to get himself killed, he can.'

'I doubt Stirling would agree with that. Henry has no experience of this.'

Henry drew himself to his full height and puffed his thin chest.

'I removed Stark and Thorpe,' he said.

Jackson nodded. 'I'd wondered about that. They wouldn't have made the mistake of attacking those poker players. It was too obvious.'

Henry beamed and patted his forehead. 'Using your head is better than using your gun.'

'In that you're right. But you'll need to use your gun to survive this.' Jackson strode across the barn to Henry. He pointed to the rifle he clutched. 'You know how to use it?'

'I reckon so.'

'Mind if I give you some advice – and advice that might keep you alive?'

Henry patted his rifle. 'Go on.'

Jackson nodded. He glanced away, then clubbed Henry across the jaw for him to sprawl on the ground. He stood over him but Henry's head lolled.

'My advice is to keep your head down, boy, and you'll live.' He turned to Zachary. 'You got a problem with that?'

Zachary laughed. 'Nope. You were right. The kid

132

would just get himself killed. And now I'm bored with arguing about who'll kill Wendell. So just stay out of my way.'

Zachary stalked to the wall facing the house. He edged to a collapsed section of the wall and knelt beside it.

Jackson joined him by the wall. 'We both have reasons to want Wendell dead. I don't care if you get him or if I get him. But we shouldn't get in each other's way.'

Zachary glanced around the wall, then darted his head back in. He nodded and glanced back at Jackson.

'Sounds a decent deal, but take this advice – three against two may look good odds, but as we're facing Wendell's gunslinger, they ain't.'

As Jackson nodded, hoof beats thundered outside the barn. He edged to the side, stood on a collapsed section of wall, and glanced over the top of the wall. He smiled.

'You may be right, but two against four is even better odds.'

Zachary joined Jackson and peered over the wall too.

Two hundred yards back from the house, Sheriff Cassidy Yates galloped down the trail.

Zachary snorted. 'Your eyesight ain't what it used to be, old-timer. I make those odds four against four.'

Jackson lifted his head to peer down the trail. He winced.

From further down the trail, Cassidy urged his horse

for more speed. Behind him Thorpe and Stark were closing.

A bullet hurtled over his head, this time closer than their previous shot.

Cassidy gritted his teeth and leaned back to fire a speculative shot. It didn't slow the men chasing him.

They fired again and, with a cry of almost human pain, his horse reared, then slid to the side, throwing Cassidy to the ground.

He rolled and came to a long, skidding halt in a huge cloud of dust.

Now only fifty yards away the gunslingers bore down on him, spurring their horses for extra speed.

With no cover but his dying horse, Cassidy leapt to his horse's side and rolled behind it. He leaned his gun hand on its still twitching shank and fired up, then ducked as Stark rode over him, leaping at the last second.

The trailing hoofs whistled over Cassidy's head, but he fell to the ground, rolled, and came up on one knee to fire at the rider's back.

He got in a wild shot before Stark turned and peppered gunfire at him. With no choice, Cassidy threw himself back to roll over his horse and between its legs. Bullets ripped into the horse's hide.

Gunfire sounded from another direction.

Cassidy thought Thorpe was outflanking him and he swung up ready to return fire, but Stirling Fontana was dashing towards him, blasting at Stark and Thorpe.

The gunslinger's horses reared and they dragged them back, then dashed away. In unison they dismounted and hunkered down behind a rock pile, fifty yards from Cassidy and slightly further from the barn and house.

Stirling skidded to a halt and with a fluid motion that belied his years vaulted the horse to join Cassidy.

'Don't like the look of your cover,' Stirling murmured.

'All I got.'

'Got to ask you, Cassidy – are you here to protect Wendell?'

Cassidy glanced at the rock pile behind which Stark and Thorpe had hid, then nodded.

'I have to protect him, but I ain't sure whether to arrest him too. I'm planning to unearth the truth.'

'You should know the truth by now. Wendell killed Ben McAlister and—'

'I'm not investigating that,' Cassidy snapped. 'I'm investigating what's happened in my town over the last few days. I have a murdered family and a dead old-timer. I'm here to find answers to that.'

'So you didn't run us out of Monotony to settle our differences?'

'Not exactly. I just ensured that your feud didn't waste more innocent lives. Out here is the best place to resolve this. Five deaths are enough.'

'Six. They killed Wayne too.'

Cassidy winced. 'You have evidence that it was Wendell?'

'It was his men.' Stirling gestured at the rock pile. 'You can tell what they're like. They're murderers who don't care who they aim at – even sheriffs.'

'They're bodyguards. They do what they must to

135

protect their charge. I ain't liking that when I'm on the receiving end, but I understand it.'

Stirling glanced over the dead horse. Nobody was visible in either the house or the barn. The new arrivals had hidden themselves well.

'So what are you planning to do?'

Cassidy roved his gun from side to side, looking for any movement.

'I intend to ask Wendell some questions.'

'He's killed one lawman. He won't baulk at killing another. You may be keeping an open mind, but listen to this – don't trust Wendell. He's a devious, conniving—'

'I know your view on Wendell.' Cassidy glanced at Stirling. 'As I keep telling you, I'm a different kind of lawman to what you were. I ask questions. If I don't like the answers, I revert to the gun, but I look for other solutions.'

For long moments Stirling stayed silent. He sighed.

'You're a decent man, Cassidy. But you're wasting your decency out here. Wendell ain't worth it.'

'I reckon any man is.' With his gun Cassidy gestured to the rock pile behind which Stark and Thorpe were hiding. 'I know how useful they are with a gun, but how good is Wendell? I ain't seen him pack one.'

'He ain't fast.' Stirling sighed. 'He's worse.'

'Nothing's worse than fast.'

'There is. He's devious. Wendell will say anything to get you to drop your guard. Then he'll kill you without flinching.'

'Devious,' Cassidy muttered. 'Then I'll use that against him.'

'How?'

By way of an answer Cassidy raised his eyebrows and added two shells to his gun.

'We have a problem,' he hollered, lifting his head above the horse's flank. He counted to five. 'I said, we have a problem.'

'Yup,' Wendell shouted from the house.

'I'm here to sort it.'

'I have no quarrel with you, Sheriff Yates.'

'And I have no quarrel with you, Wendell Moon.'

'Then what are you here for?'

'I'm here for Zachary Forester.'

'He's in the barn,' Wendell shouted. 'You're welcome to him.'

'What you want with me, Sheriff?' Zachary shouted from the barn.

'I'm taking you back to Monotony to answer some questions.'

Zachary snorted. 'Ask them here.'

'This is a fraught situation. But you have nothing to worry about if you're innocent.'

'Innocent of what?'

'The murder of Chase Longhorn.'

'Who in tarnation is he?'

'Stirling Fontana said you quarrelled with him. His death three days ago seems mighty odd.'

'I wasn't in town three days ago.'

Cassidy glanced back at Stirling, who smiled. Cassidy cleared his throat.

'Then you and I need to talk back in Monotony. If

that's true, I'll let you go.'

Zachary snorted. 'I have business with Wendell.'

'Not today you haven't. After you and I have cleared our problem, you're free to conclude your business, provided you do it peacefully. I'll stand now and walk towards you. Don't be foolish or you'll regret it.'

'Let's hope,' Stirling whispered, grabbing Cassidy's arm as he moved to rise, 'that Zachary ain't as stupid as he looks.'

Cassidy nodded and stood. With a large stride he paced over his horse. He kept his hands high with his gun pointed up as he strode towards the barn.

Wendell and Lance peered at him over the house's wall. Stark and Thorpe glared at him from the rock pile.

Cassidy nodded to them, receiving a short nod from Wendell and a bemused headshake from Stark and Thorpe.

At the barn he stopped five paces back from the wall.

'I'm coming in.'

To Zachary's nod, he climbed through a gap in the wall. He glanced at the youngster sprawled against the wall, then tipped his hat to Jackson.

'What you playing at, Sheriff?' Zachary whispered.

'Holster your gun,' Cassidy said.

Zachary glanced at Jackson, who nodded. With a shake of his head Zachary followed Cassidy's orders.

'What now?'

'Get on your horse and I'll escort you to Monotony.'

As Zachary frowned, Jackson whispered something to him. Zachary snorted and with Cassidy behind him he climbed over the wall. They stalked to the two horses behind the barn.

'When we going for Wendell?' Zachary whispered from the corner of his mouth.

'Be quiet,' Cassidy muttered, then lowered his voice to a whisper. 'We ain't.'

'Then what are we doing?'

Cassidy leapt on the spare horse and waited until Zachary mounted his. He edged his horse around the barn to face the house.

'I'm testing a theory.' Cassidy tipped back his hat. 'My problem is I don't know whether to arrest Wendell or just protect him. But with you out of the way, the situation will be calmer and the solution closer. If Stirling and Jackson take on Wendell, I'll protect him, but if Wendell's gunslingers fire at them, I'll arrest him. Got a feeling I'll find out which one I'm doing in the next few moments.'

'I ain't siding with that,' Zachary muttered.

'You got no choice.' Cassidy held out his hand. 'So hand over your gunbelt and we'll ride out of here real slow.'

Zachary glanced away, muttering to himself.

Then he yanked on the reins, pulled his horse to the side, and urged it to gallop straight at the house.

'Wendell Moon!' he roared. 'You're breathing your last.'

In ten long strides he reached the house. With a huge cry behind him Cassidy followed.

Zachary tugged on the reins urging his horse to

vault into the house. He landed inside, the huge leap nearly tumbling him over his horse's head.

Inside Wendell and Lance flew to the ground to avoid the pounding hoofs.

In two long paces the horse surged across the house, but just as it leapt at the other wall, Zachary hurled himself to the ground. He landed on his side and rolled twice.

Five seconds later, Cassidy cleared the wall, a volley of gunshots from Stark and Thorpe peppering into the wall behind him. He threw himself to the ground, rolled, and slammed to a halt against the wall.

From the ground Zachary ripped gunfire at Wendell.

Wendell threw himself flat, lead cannoning into the wall above his tumbling form.

With his back pressed against the wall, Lance fired at Zachary, catching him with a shot to the shoulder.

Cassidy leapt to his feet and dashed at Lance.

Lance spun on his heel but walked into Cassidy's flailing fist. He staggered back, then folded as Zachary blasted a slug into his guts from the ground. Lance righted himself, fired two shots into Zachary, then fell to his side.

Cassidy glanced at the still Lance, then the unarmed Wendell. He dashed to Zachary's side, but the outlaw wasn't breathing. With an irritated grunt at having used him to create this situation, he glanced over the wall. Outside more gunfire blasted between Wendell's gunslingers, Stirling and Jackson.

Scrambling sounded behind him. He turned to face Wendell.

Wendell stood over Lance; his former protector's gun aimed at Cassidy's head, his blank eyes gleaming.

'Put that down,' Cassidy muttered.

'I have a right to defend myself,' Wendell croaked. 'And as Lance can't do that, I can use his gun.'

'I didn't believe you killed a lawman.' Cassidy took a long pace forward. 'But that belief is eroding fast.'

Wendell backed up a pace to slam into the wall.

'I don't want to harm you, Sheriff. But I ain't sure what your intentions are.'

Cassidy raised his arms a mite, turning his gun towards Wendell.

'I had a difficult decision to make, but now I've made it. I'm taking you into protective custody *and* I'll be formally asking you some questions.'

'You have me wrong, Cassidy. What happened fifteen years ago was—'

'Only thing on my mind is the deaths of the last few days. And a few minutes ago your men tried to kill me. A man has a right to bodyguards but not ones who shoot at lawmen.'

Wendell nodded. 'I didn't give them permission to do that.'

'Right now I don't know what to believe.' Cassidy took another pace towards Wendell and swung his gun another inch towards him. 'But it's hard to come to an honest assessment when a man has a gun on you.'

Wendell gulped and glanced from his gun to the gun in Cassidy's hand. He lowered his head and let the gun swing down, then with his head still down he underhanded it to Cassidy's feet.

With his left hand Cassidy lifted the gun.

'Obliged.'

'Like I said, you have me wrong.' Wendell looked up and spread his arms wide. His blank eyes widened. 'I'm in your protection now. You won't get any tricks from me.'

CHAPTER 17

'You are under arrest,' Cassidy muttered.

'I have no problem with that,' Wendell said, his former grin returning. 'Phillip will see that I only answer to relevant crimes. And as there are none, I'll be free within hours.'

Cassidy nodded and stalked to the wall. Outside sporadic gunfire still sounded. He peered over the wall, then turned to Wendell.

'We have an impasse.'

Wendell nodded. 'We can deal with that.'

'Then start by ordering Stark and Thorpe to throw out their guns.'

'I could, but they won't when they don't know I'm safe and when I'm facing those gun-toting ex-lawmen.'

'Stirling, Jackson,' Cassidy hollered. 'I have Wendell under arrest *and* in my protection. He's returning to Monotony to face whatever crimes are his responsibility. This is over, so throw out your guns.'

'No way,' Jackson shouted.

'Like Jackson says,' Stirling shouted. 'No way – not with Wendell's men here.'

Wendell joined Cassidy at the wall. With a shared nod they peered over the top.

'Stark, Thorpe,' Wendell shouted, 'throw out your guns.'

'Get those ex-lawmen to do it first,' Stark shouted.

Cassidy sighed. 'We'll do this one at a time. Stark, throw out your gun. When it hits the ground, Stirling will throw out his. Whichever one of you reneges on that will answer to me.'

'Do it, Stark,' Wendell shouted.

A gun arced from behind the rock pile. It skidded to a halt.

Long seconds passed. A gun hurtled out from behind the dead horse.

'That's good,' Cassidy shouted. 'Now we deal with Thorpe and Jackson – same procedure.'

A gun slammed into the ground before Thorpe's position. A further gun appeared from the barn.

'And the other one,' Wendell shouted. 'There's two men in the barn.'

'You heard him, Jackson, the other gun too.'

A rifle flew end over end until it landed before the house.

With Wendell before him Cassidy edged over a gap in the wall and into the open.

One by one the other men stood. They glanced at each other, then strode into the clearing before the house to form a loose circle.

'Jackson, where's the other man?' Cassidy asked.

Jackson glanced at Stirling, then shook his head.

'He ain't coming.'

Cassidy nodded. 'We're returning to Monotony. When Wendell is behind bars, we'll talk again.' He turned to Stark. 'Head for your horse first.'

Stark glared back, then lowered his head.

As Cassidy turned to direct Thorpe, Stark grabbed his pocket. Cassidy saw the glint of steel emerge from Stark's pocket. He fell to one knee and blasted lead at Stark. His shot was wild, but Stark's returning shot whistled over Cassidy's head.

Beside him, Stirling dashed for his gun and with a long dive leapt at it, sliding across the ground as he pulled it into his grasp.

Thorpe charged for his gun.

Jackson judged the distance to his own gun, then leapt to his side to knock Thorpe to the ground.

On his knee, Cassidy steadied his stance. Another bullet blasted from Stark's gun, the tiny weapon's inaccuracy saving Cassidy, but Cassidy's first aimed shot ripped through Stark's shoulder and a second shot thundered into his chest, knocking him to the ground.

Cassidy jumped to his feet, wrapped an arm around Wendell's neck, and dragged him back a pace. He aimed his gun at the fighting Thorpe and Jackson.

Jackson shrugged free from Thorpe, but received a solid slug to the jaw, which knocked him flat.

Thorpe dashed for his gun, but slid to a halt when he saw that Stirling and Cassidy already had guns on him.

Cassidy smiled. 'Looks like you can join Wendell in custody.'

In five shuffled paces, with Wendell held firmly, Cassidy edged to Thorpe's gun. He holstered his gun and released Wendell to grab it.

As he knelt, Thorpe charged at him, a bullet from Stirling hurtling over his shoulder. Caught in a moment of indecision between grabbing Thorpe's gun and clutching Wendell, Cassidy wavered. Then he jumped to his feet and lunged for Wendell, but his grasp closed on air as Wendell scurried away.

Thorpe leapt at Cassidy, catching him around the chest and pushing him back. Thorpe crashed on top of Cassidy, but with a thrust of his shoulders, Cassidy bucked his assailant and the two men rolled to the side, each trying to press the other man's head into the dirt. A thundering blow to the jaw knocked Cassidy to the side.

Cassidy rolled free and carried the roll on expecting Stirling to shoot Thorpe now, but when the shot didn't come, he stopped his roll and looked back.

Wendell and Stirling were struggling over Stirling's gun, the weapon held high above their heads as they each tried to swing it down. Thorpe was scrambling for his gun.

Cassidy leapt to his feet and, with a running dive, leapt on Thorpe's back. He pummelled him to the ground and, kneeling on his back, slammed Thorpe's forehead into the solid earth. Thorpe slackened, then lay still.

Cassidy rolled off his back. Ten feet away Stirling lay on his back, clutching his jaw.

With Stirling's gun held before him, Wendell was backing into the barn.

Cassidy rolled his shoulders and stood. With a slow pull of his gun he strode towards Wendell.

'Watch out!' Stirling shouted.

Cassidy turned on the hip, his gun barrel arcing towards Thorpe.

Thorpe leapt and slid across the ground. His outstretched fingers closed on his gun. With no choice, Cassidy fired a single shot, the lead blasting Thorpe in the neck.

Thorpe crumpled.

With his upper lip curled in distaste Cassidy watched, confirming that this time Thorpe wasn't acting, then turned.

But Wendell had now backed into the barn.

As no horses were close to the barn, Cassidy collected Stirling. They checked on Jackson and Cassidy slapped his face until he was conscious.

'Wendell,' Jackson murmured.

'He's going nowhere. Either he gives himself up or he doesn't.' Cassidy stood and backed away from both men. 'But I'll be taking him into custody until I can resolve everything that's happened around here. We do this the right way from now on. Vengeance is never the answer. And today is no exception.'

Stirling nodded. 'You're in charge, Cassidy. We won't oppose you.'

Jackson shook himself and rubbed his forehead.

'Yeah, I suppose so,' he said. 'Where is he?'

'In the barn.'

Jackson winced and glanced at Stirling.

'Henry,' he whispered.

'What?' Stirling snapped.

'Henry is in the barn.'

'Don't be. . . .' Stirling paled and dashed for the barn.

'Who's Henry?' Cassidy asked.

'Stirling's son. He came along to help his pa, except Stirling didn't know.'

Stirling skidded to a halt at the side of the barn.

'Henry!' he roared.

Inside the barn Wendell had grabbed Henry and slammed the gun against his temple. The youngster struggled, but his eyes were clearly unfocused and his movements were stilted.

Wendell turned Henry so that he was before him. He grinned.

'Seems like this is your boy, Stirling.'

'Get off him,' Stirling muttered, speaking each word with steady menace.

'I'm all right, Pa,' Henry murmured, blinking rapidly.

'What you doing here, boy?'

Henry gulped. 'I came here to help you.'

'You damn fool!'

Henry nodded. He struggled, but finding that Wendell's grip was firm, he slumped.

'Kill him, Pa. I only came to ensure you didn't get yourself killed.'

'Stop!' Cassidy shouted, joining Stirling. 'Nobody is getting killed here. Wendell, I said I'd take you into protective custody and give you a fair hearing. And I will.'

Wendell shook his head. 'I don't trust you now, Sheriff.'

148

Wendell wrapped his arm more tightly around the youngster's neck, forcing him to stand on tiptoes.

Stirling took a long pace, but Cassidy grabbed his arm, halting him.

'Wendell,' Cassidy muttered. 'Threatening Stirling's boy ain't wise.'

'I ain't threatening him. We're just riding out of here. Five miles down the trail, I'll leave him, but only if you ain't following.'

'You ain't leaving.'

'Shut up, Cassidy,' Stirling shouted, ripping his arm from Cassidy's grasp. 'You're the lawman, but that's my boy and I decide what happens.'

Cassidy glanced at Stirling's grim expression that had aged years in a matter of seconds. He nodded.

'What have you decided?'

Stirling turned to Wendell. He pointed a firm finger at him.

'You get the chance to do what you promised. You can leave here. Five miles down the trail you leave Henry. We won't pursue you.'

'Stirling,' Jackson muttered from behind him. 'We're dealing with Wendell Moon. He's the biggest double-crossing snake in the world.'

'He is,' Stirling said, staring at Wendell. 'He'll say anything to wheedle himself out of trouble. But he knows that if he doesn't follow through with his promise, Cassidy will know what a snake he is and every lawman in the country won't rest until he swings.'

Wendell gulped. 'You got me wrong, Stirling. I'm a changed man.'

'Then prove it. You made a promise – *keep it.*'

Wendell nodded. 'I always keep my word. Now move back.'

To Wendell's short gesture with his gun, Stirling and the others backed five paces from the barn wall.

Wendell edged to the side, dragging Henry with him.

Henry struggled, but Stirling lifted a hand.

'Trust me, boy. He won't harm you.'

Henry struggled again, then let Wendell lead him over the barn wall. Wendell kept Henry held before him and facing the others as he dragged him to the horses at a steady pace.

Stirling, Jackson and Cassidy formed a line to watch them edge away. They shared a grim frown, then returned to watching Wendell's every move.

Pace by pace the two men backed away, Wendell's arm firm across Henry's neck, the gun barrel digging into his temple.

Henry's eyes were wide but he stared at his father, who returned an insistent gaze and shook his head as he mouthed calming words.

At the nearest horse, Wendell released his tight grip on Henry's neck.

Henry fell to his knees, whimpering.

Stirling advanced an involuntary pace, then lifted his hands and backed off when Wendell glared at him and dug the gun hard against Henry's temple.

Keeping his movements slow, Wendell dragged Henry to his feet. He murmured a terse command and placed Henry's right hand on the saddle. He pulled back the gun as Henry swung himself on to

150

the horse, then gestured to him to put his hands high.

Henry followed his instructions, his outstretched hands shaking.

With a last glance at Stirling and a mouthed warning, Wendell mounted the horse behind him.

But as Wendell swung his leg over the horse and was off-balance, Henry dropped his arms and thrust a bony elbow into Wendell's guts, knocking him back.

'No,' Stirling shouted, breaking into a run.

Wendell lunged, grabbing Henry around the neck and they both tumbled from the horse, landing in a heap on the other side.

With an agonized cry, Stirling hurtled for the horse, but the horse's legs floundered, blocking his way and his view of the two struggling men.

Through the pounding legs slices of the men were visible as Wendell struggled to hold down the squirming youngster. Gunmetal reflected the rays of the lowering sun as Wendell thrust the gun against Henry's chest, but with a desperate lunge the youngster knocked it away and both men rolled over each other.

Stirling dashed to the side, searching for a route to reach the struggling men, but the panicking horse blocked him.

Behind the horse dust plumed, arms and legs flailing as the younger man tried to buck the elder man from his chest.

Stirling turned and hurtled the other way, bustling into Cassidy and Jackson as they each tried to find a route to the fighting twosome.

Cassidy directed Jackson to grab the horse's reins and directed Stirling to head left while he headed right. With his head down, Stirling followed his instructions.

Henry and Wendell rolled to their feet. They flexed back and forth, the gun swinging widely over their heads. Then it slipped down between their two chests.

A gunshot blasted.

'Henry!' Stirling shouted. In desperation he ran and dived at the horse, hurling himself to the ground to skid beneath it. Hoofs thundered into his side as he scrambled on hands and feet across the ground to roll free in a wild tangle of limbs.

But Henry staggered back from the prone Wendell. In his outstretched hand he clutched Wendell's gun.

Stirling rolled to kneel on one knee, his gun drawn and aimed at Wendell's head, but Wendell lay flat, holding his chest, blood seeping through his clutching fingers.

'You got me wrong,' Wendell whispered, his voice weakening. 'I'm a changed man. You got me wrong.'

Wendell's head lolled to the side, a bubble of blood on his lips.

Henry hurled the gun away, a sob escaping as he fell to his knees and pressed his forehead to the dirt.

Wendell gave one last twitch, then stilled.

'It's over,' Stirling muttered and, with a celebratory flourish, twirled his gun back into its holster.

Jackson grabbed the horse's reins and controlled

the frightened animal, letting Cassidy join Stirling. Cassidy glared at Wendell's body.

'Seems like it is,' he said.

Stirling jumped to his feet. 'You got any problem with my boy?'

'Nope,' Cassidy said, tipping back his hat. 'Wendell had a gun on an unarmed man. Henry was just defending himself.'

'Good.' Stirling stormed to his sobbing son and dragged him to his feet. He slapped him hard across the cheek, causing him to fall back.

'What's that for?' Henry screeched, holding his cheek.

'That's for disobeying me,' Stirling roared, standing over him with his fists raised. 'I told you to stay at the farm.'

'I just . . . I just. . . .'

Stirling slapped him hard across the shoulder.

'And that's for siding with that outlaw, and that's for. . . .'

Stirling's fists slackened and he hung his head. He fell to his knees and grabbed Henry around the chest, hugging him close.

Cassidy nodded to Jackson and they both backed away from the two men.

'With Wendell dead we've finished our business here,' Jackson said, 'but we'll stay as long as you still have questions.'

'I still have plenty of questions.' Cassidy sighed. 'But I only need to ask them of myself. I created this situation to uncover the truth, but I didn't do that and I failed to protect a man who was in my custody.'

Jackson shook his head. 'You're too hard on your-self, Cassidy. Just remember, trust nothing that Wendell said.'

'I'll make up my own mind.'

'You're your own man. You're entitled to run your territory the way you see fit. But just take my advice.' Jackson sighed. 'It came from someone who used to be a lawman.'

With that Jackson tipped his hat and strode to Stirling's side. He pulled him to his feet, then pulled Henry up too.

Cassidy watched the three men share a round of backslapping. Then Stirling stood over Wendell's body and said the words that he'd promised he'd say fifteen years ago.

Cassidy didn't stay to hear them.

CHAPTER 18

Two weeks after Wendell Moon's death, Sheriff Cassidy Yates sat in his office, letting the afternoon pass peacefully. He'd completed his investigation into the events that had occurred during Wendell's three days in Monotony and had resolved most of his concerns.

He'd now received positive identification of the bodies at the Whittler farm. Aside from the Whittler family, the other men were petty outlaws and it was safe to assume that Zachary Forester had enrolled them into a gang to track down Wendell.

The brutality of the Whittler family's demise meant they were this gang's final victims.

While Zachary waylaid Tom McDonald and Bert Caster, Thorpe and Stark had to have killed Wayne Stone – an alibi they couldn't offer.

Phillip Tannin's sneaky dispatch of Deputy Giles suggested that he had killed Chase Longhorn.

Cassidy accepted that he'd never receive confirmation of this. After Phillip had fled Monotony he had headed to Beaver Ridge. But Marshal Devine was waiting for him, and after Phillip made the mistake of pulling his concealed weapon, he didn't live long enough to explain himself.

But one matter still nagged at Cassidy.

Although Stirling and Jackson were convinced of Wendell's lying nature, Cassidy couldn't link any of the deaths in Monotony to him, nor could he find anywhere to even start investigating Sheriff McAlister's death fifteen years ago.

His investigations had confirmed that Wendell Moon was a businessman with connections that stretched to the Pacific. Over the last three years he had successfully speculated over land purchases.

Cassidy didn't find any complaints about his business practices.

Although Phillip Tannin was also involved in Wendell's business dealings and he had killed Chase Longhorn and Deputy Giles, that still didn't implicate Wendell.

As each piece of information arrived to complete the picture of the last few days, Wendell's continual protestations of innocence increasingly appeared true.

Cassidy now suspected that his original feelings were right – Wendell Moon was a man with a past who had gone straight. But because of his past, he had needed protection and had sought it from men who dealt with guns and were prepared to use them.

The worst sin he had committed was to look the other way when those men had meted out violence.

Failure to stop violence wasn't a crime.

But worse than Wendell being innocent was the

terrible fact that Cassidy had failed to protect a man in a situation that he had engineered.

Such an admission gnawed at his gut.

'Message over the wire,' Deputy Hearst said, wandering into the office and breaking Cassidy's brooding.

'What does it say?' Cassidy asked, looking up from his desk.

Hearst glanced at the paper he clutched in his right hand.

'Five foot two and plump.'

Cassidy chuckled. The chuckle grew into a laugh. He suppressed the laugh and held out a hand for the note.

Cassidy read the note, confirming that this was all it said.

'Five foot two and plump,' he said and threw the telegram to the desk. He leaned back in his chair and puffed his chest.

'From your reaction that sounds like good news,' Hearst said.

'It sure is.'

'But it doesn't mean much to me when I don't know what question you asked.' Hearst considered Cassidy's beaming smile, then joined in the smiling. 'You telling me what it was?'

Cassidy let out his breath with a long sigh and nodded.

'The problem I've had is that Stirling, Frank and the rest told me that every word Wendell ever uttered was a lie. But as far as I could tell, everything Wendell said to me was the truth and as such, he was the changed man he claimed to be. But if I could prove that just one thing he told me was a lie, everything else would collapse, because if he could look me in the eye and lie once, he could lie about anything.'

'And that message proves something Wendell said was a lie?'

'It sure does. He told me he spent twelve years in Leavenworth jail under his real name, Miles Coleman. While he was there, he met a man who suggested a legitimate line of business. When they came out they worked together and went straight.'

'But you checked that out. It did happen just the way Wendell said it happened.'

'Yup. Miles Coleman did serve twelve years for killing a man over a poker game and Phillip Tannin also served three years in the same jail at the same time for fraud. For all I know Miles could have met Phillip in jail and planned how to earn an honest living when they came out. His story seemed to check out. But Wendell looked me in the eye and told me a lie.'

Hearst contemplated Cassidy. He nodded.

'You asked the jail for a description of Miles Coleman.'

'Yup.' Cassidy waved the wired message. 'And that description is five foot two and plump. That doesn't describe Wendell Moon. But it does describe the man we called Phillip Tannin.'

'Most unfortunate. It'd seem that . . .' Hearst rubbed his brow. 'It doesn't make sense. Did Wendell serve a jail sentence or was he always free? And who was Phillip? And. . . .'

Cassidy shrugged. 'It doesn't matter. Wendell lied and he did it well because I believed him, just like I believed everything else he said.'

'But not any more?'

'Nope.'

'We need to get word to Stirling and Jackson. They need to know the truth.'

'Don't need to. They were well ahead of me on everything all along.' Cassidy strode to the window and looked out at the bustling road beyond. 'They're lawmen.'